COOPER

FEDERAL PROTECTION AGENCY

BOOK FOUR

BY EVIE RILEY

Cooper

Federal Protection Agency

Book Four

Copyright © 2022

Evie Riley

Second Edition

ISBN: 978-1-77357-669-5

Published by Naughty Nights Press LLC

Cover Art By Willsin Rowe

COOPER

The right path can save a life...

Growing up in foster care, the only true friends Cooper Jones had were the black hat hackers at the community center. At eighteen, after being caught by the government for hacking into Homeland Security, The Agent in Charge, impressed by Coop's skills, determined he needed to work for the government instead of hacking them. That Agent saved him from a life of crime, and almost certainly saved his life.

Now an analyst and hacker for Homeland Security, Coop prefers to be behind a computer to fight his battles. Recently scooped up by the Federal Protection Agency, he is a valuable asset to the team.

Detective Jonah West has dedicated his life to helping the people of Baton Rouge and he doesn't like it when criminals get to go free on a technicality. He spends countless hours every day being the best police officer he can to make sure that doesn't happen often. The downside to a cop's life is that his twelve-year-old son, Drew, spends much of his time alone with only his computer for entertainment. When his house is broken into and Drew comes up missing, Jonah contacts the FPA and asks them for help. Jonah is willing to pull out all the stops if it means getting his son back.

Can Coop and Jonah keep Drew safe while they track down the kidnappers, and will their growing closeness mean they have a future together?

CHAPTER ONE

Jonah

MY WHOLE BODY was sore. It had been a long night at work. Hell, it had been a long week.

I hated doing shift work, it was always hard getting used to going from days to nights without much notice in between. That was the life of a detective, though. Everyone had to take turns working overnights so we could all get the chance to enjoy sleeping in our own bed at night and being outside during daylight hours. The trick was, though, when I caught a case, it wasn't like I could just go home when my shift was over.

I worked in the homicide division, so when a case came in, we only had forty-eight hours to try and solve it before our chances of finding the killer went down drastically. Which meant it was quite often a lot of long hours, working all day and night just to try to get justice for the victim. Today, I had been going for thirty-six hours straight and I was in desperate need of some sleep.

It was eight in the morning when I pulled into my driveway. It was Wednesday, though, so I couldn't just head up to bed. I had to get my twelve year old son ready for school.

Andrew, or Drew, as he preferred, was the reason I worked so hard. I wanted to make sure these streets were safer for him, because I knew all too soon he would be off on his own and carving out his own path in this world. I wanted to try and make it at least a little bit safer for him to be out on the streets at night. My greatest fear was getting a call to go out to a crime scene only to discover the victim was my son. It was something I knew I would have to face when his mother got pregnant. I wasn't really sure I was ready to be a father at that point in my life, but I knew I couldn't walk away from him.

My whole life, I had tried to fit within the right box. The box that society said I was supposed to fit into. I had always been athletic. I played on the football team, and I was on the basketball team, too. I loved playing sports, I still do. I was a guy's guy. However, I was a guy's guy who liked to look at other guys naked.

I knew I was gay from the age of twelve. I knew it wasn't normal to enjoy watching the other guys change in the locker rooms or see them showering. I was well aware that I enjoyed it too much. However, I was also well aware that the other guys would never be cool with being around a gay man. I couldn't be gay, not back then, so I did what every other guy was doing. I dated girls. I had sex with girls, even though it wasn't really who I wanted to be with, and I told myself that was going to have to be good enough. I suppressed my gay self in favor of fitting in where society expected me to.

I was eighteen when I joined the police

academy and once more, I was faced with an environment that wasn't open minded and welcoming of gay men. I continued to hide and I even got marricd to Melissa. When I was twenty-three, she gave birth to my son.

I was twenty-nine when I finally decided I couldn't do it anymore. I couldn't keep living the lie. I couldn't keep my desires at bay. I couldn't keep having sex with my wife and wishing it was a man underneath me. I just couldn't do it anymore.

So, one night when my son was six, I told Melissa that I was gay and wanted a divorce. She didn't handle it well. I knew she wouldn't. She tried telling me that I was just going through a phase. That I was confused. That I enjoyed having sex with her. After all, we had a son. She didn't appreciate it when I pointed out that I only got off on the friction of having sex with her and the vivid fantasies I would have while we had sex. Fantasies of a guy underneath me, whimpering and begging for more. She really didn't appreciate that part. Though, in her defense, I shouldn't have said it, but I was so sick of listening to her going on and on about how I was confused. I wasn't confused. I was just sick and tired of living in that small closet. After twenty-nine years, I had every right to live my life for myself. I wanted to explore my own sexuality, for the first time in my life.

I knew we would get divorced. It was going to be a very easy divorce, because there was no fixing us. I was into men and so was she. There was nothing either of us could do or say that would ever change that.

I had truly hoped that we would be able to co-parent and be friends. I knew it wouldn't be right away, but Melissa had always been open minded and okay with different sexual orientations. She had male and female friends who were gay. I figured once the dust settled and the hard feelings had passed, that she would be okay with me, too. I was very wrong. She was okay with other people. She was not okay with me. Not her husband. Nope. She had never been okay with me since the day I told her I was gay.

The divorce was simple. She signed it almost immediately and she wanted to avoid having to go to court. I thought it was great, that we were going to be able to get along and co-parent, that she had been taking this all so well. And then, it was time to work out the custody agreement and she ghosted us.

She had signed over full custody to me for Drew. According to the document she sent me along with the custody paperwork, she couldn't stand to look at either one of us. She felt that Drew would only remind her of the worst years of her life. Of the deception that I had put her through. She felt like I had somehow conned her into loving me and giving me a child. As if I was some sort of con man using her for her money and a kid. She wanted nothing to do with me and, even worse, she wanted nothing to do with Drew.

We hadn't seen or heard from her since that day. Six years, now. Not a single fucking word. Drew never received a phone call, no text message, no birthday card or Christmas card. Nothing. Having to explain to my son at the age of six where his mother was and why she wasn't coming back wasn't something I ever thought I would have to do.

At the age of six, he didn't understand why his own mother wasn't around. It wasn't like she hadn't been around for his whole life. When she was there, she had been a loving and doting mother. She was always helping with his playgroups and then with his school. She was on the PTA and spearheaded every fundraiser and bake sale. She was an active mom and I thought she loved being a mom.

I knew we were still young when we had him. She was twenty-two, but I figured we both had our jobs and we were responsible adults. I never missed going out to bars and clubs and partying all night. I didn't think she missed it, either. She never showed any signs of missing that life.

But at the first chance she had to leave and wipe the slate clean, she did.

For months afterward, Drew would sit in front of the windows in the living room, staring out at the driveway, waiting for her to come home. The first birthday and Christmas were hard. He was so confident that his mother would come by for them and when she didn't, there was no amount of comfort that I could give him that made him feel better.

That first Christmas was heartbreaking for me. He ran down the stairs Christmas morning and completely ignored the presents under the tree. He sat up on his knees on the couch and looked out the window and waited for

Melissa to come over. When I tried to get him to open his presents from Santa, he refused and said he would do it when Mommy got there. All day, he sat there on his knees just watching the driveway, and every time a car drove by, he got his hopes up that it was Melissa. He went to bed that night crying his heart out and with not a single present opened.

I had to call my parents and they drove fourteen hours to come down to spend a few days with us. Only when his grandparents had arrived did he finally feel like opening presents.

My mom was amazing, because she had brought everything to cook for a full Christmas dinner. It had been a hard day, but we all got through it. Drew had gotten through it.

I had to hand it to my parents, they

were older and they generally had traditional beliefs, but they supported me in being gay. It was a bit shaky at first, but when they discovered that Melissa had abandoned Drew, they were outraged. My father called her a closed minded bitch for not being able to accept me as gay and raise our son together. They were old fashioned, but to them abandoning your child was a far worse crime than being gay and raising one.

We didn't talk about my sexual orientation and I hadn't really brought a guy over to their house. We kind of had a bit of a Don't Ask, Don't Tell rule, but that was okay with me. It wasn't like I wanted to talk to them about my boyfriends, anyway.

As I walked inside the house, I was fully prepared to see Drew running around and grabbing the last of his things. I didn't have a babysitter for him when I worked nights. He was twelve and I knew he was responsible enough to handle being on his own. It wasn't like I went into work at five or six o'clock at night. I went to work at ten and he was in bed for ten-thirty. When he was younger, I'd had a babysitter, but now we both felt he was old enough to sleep alone in the house with all of the windows and doors locked.

I also had a security system with an alarm on every door and window so he was perfectly safe once he was in the house. And he wasn't old enough to go sneaking out at night. That would be something I knew I was going to have to deal with when he was around sixteen. Thankfully, I had at least four years before that would happen.

Drew was also very mature and responsible for his age. I never had to worry about him doing something incredibly stupid. He made it easy to trust him alone.

What I didn't expect to see when I walked into my home was the obvious signs of a struggle. The house was a mess and the further I walked in, the more worried I became. There were lamps shattered on the floor, the coffee table was broken, furniture was turned over, the picture frames on the walls were crooked and some were on the floor, the glass broken. What had my heart stopping, though, was seeing the directional blood drops leading from the living room to the front door.

"Drew!" I screamed as I ran from room

to room, trying to find my son.

The detective in me knew I was being an idiot. I was running around an obvious crime scene, potentially destroying evidence, but I had to find my son. He could be hurt somewhere in my own home and I was not about to leave him injured on his own while I waited for the crime scene techs to get there.

I searched every room in the whole house, but Drew wasn't there. My son wasn't there. I could feel panic starting to claw at my throat, but I fought through it. Me panicking was not going to find my son any faster.

I had to focus.

I had to work the scene and follow the steps.

I had to think.

I had to follow proper procedures.

I sucked in a deep breath and let it out slowly. With a shaky hand, I pulled out my cell phone and called the kidnapping in. The fact that I had to actually call my own son's kidnapping in tore at my heart.

With the crime reported, though, I then turned to calling every single one of my son's friends to see if they had heard from him since last night. I needed to know if he had been missing only an hour or two, or if he had been missing all night. Just like with murders, the first forty-eight hours in a kidnapping were the most crucial. If we didn't find him within forty-eight hours of the time of his disappearance, we might never find him. Or worse, I might find him dead.

I had to work this case, but I knew there was no way in hell my boss would let me. It was too personal. I was too close to it. I understood that, I did, but I was not going to sit on my ass and let this son of a bitch have my son.

No one knew these streets better than I did.

I had informants and contacts in the Southside. They wouldn't talk to any cop but me, and if they knew my own son was missing they would help me. But in order to get them to help, I would need access to this case so I could point them in the right direction. And the only way I was going to get access to this case was if I was working it.

The second the patrol cars pulled in, I gave them my statement before I got into my car and headed off for the one place that I knew could help.

The Federal Protection Agency.

I had helped them with one case two

months ago and they all seemed like stand up guys. They were all capable of stopping a serial killer. I knew they were making a rather impressive name for themselves within their area of expertise. They focused on crimes against children and my son's case was exactly within the realm of their specialty. I needed their help and I knew I would have a better chance at convincing them to let me work the case with them than I did with my own boss.

I also knew they didn't have to follow the letter of the law. They had immunity; they could break the law and do whatever they had to do to get their cases closed. To save children. I needed that right now. I needed to know that someone would kick in the door to save my son even without a warrant. I needed to know that we wouldn't have to wait around for evidence or for a judge to issue a warrant if we didn't have anything solid.

The FPA working the case increased the odds of my son being found and that was all that mattered.

The second I pulled up to the building, I ran inside and up to their office floor. I strolled right into their conference room without stopping. I saw some new faces as I walked by, but I ignored them. I needed to speak with Mason. He was the only person who mattered right now. I knocked on his office door before I walked in without waiting to be granted entry.

Mason was in charge of the Agency and his K9 partner, Koda, was never far from his side. I didn't have the pleasure of working with him on the serial killer case. He had been in the hospital with his boyfriend, Jarod. Their serial killer, Marcus Long, who was also a detective at the time, had been killing young teenage boys and torturing them before leaving them in a dumpster.

The Agency had been brought in by a FBI Profiler, Knox Hunter, to help after he'd had nothing on the killer for three months. At the last crime scene, Long had planted a bomb designed to hurt Ryzen, a man who worked for the Agency and was ordered to protect Knox. In that blast, Ryzen had ended up with some bruised ribs, but Jarod had taken a large shard of metal to his stomach. He had to have part of his liver removed and had been placed on medical leave, followed by desk duty for three months.

"Detective West, what brings you by unannounced?" Mason asked.

"My twelve year old son, Drew, has been kidnapped. I need your help."

I was hoping, I was praying, that he would say yes. That he would takc this case over and then I could maybe take a breath, finally. I knew the guys in the Baton Rouge Kidnapping Division were good, don't get me wrong. The problem was, they had too many cases and not enough detectives. The Crime Lab was backed up, too, so any evidence that could help you find a missing child was delayed by weeks, sometimes months. They weren't fast at solving cases and that wasn't their fault, but I wasn't going to wait for months to find my son. I was going to find him before he was killed. There was simply no other option.

"Tell me everything," Mason said, and the tightness that had been wrapped around my throat started to loosen up, just a tiny bit.

CHAPTER TWO

Cooper

I HEADED INTO the conference room to see that Sebastian, Damien, and Max were the only ones there.

I had no idea what the case would be, but I knew we had a new one. It would be different for us, because for the most part, we had been working cases all together and one at a time. Within the past couple of weeks, though, the team had picked up some new guys and we were able to work more than one case at a time.

We currently had two cases going on. The first one was a drug trafficking ring that was using young kids as mules, dealers, and cooks. Ryzen, Roland, Rafe, and Hollingsworth were currently working that one. Jarod was also helping out on desk duty and I knew Mason was good to jump in should we need it. He had a shit load of paperwork he was stuck doing, because with everything one of his guys on the team did, he had to fill out paperwork for it.

The second case we had on the go was an underground brothel and strip club using underage girls as their workers. That was being handled by the new guys, Kruze, Gabe, and Deke. I didn't know much about them, but they had only started working with the team in the past two weeks. They seemed like good guys and Mason handpicked them himself, so I had to trust his judgment.

I was still the only computer guy, though, so I was working both cases and running whatever tracing they needed. Thankfully, they could run names themselves, but I was the one working any security cameras and doing a deeper dive into their victims and suspects. We needed another computer tech, another hacker, who could work the cases as well, because soon enough it would be too much for me to handle. Not that I minded being kept busy, but I had to sleep at some point, too.

"We got another case?" I asked as I slid into my chair.

"Mason didn't give logistics, just asked if we could come in and help with a local case," Damien answered.

"You know, with the amount of times you get brought in here, you really should consider moving here," I commented.

Damien, Sebastian, and Max were private detectives who worked for their own company in Gaithersburg, Maryland. We would often call them to come out and help us when we needed more guys. They came down for the last case a week ago to help with a major raid and had stuck around to help with the paperwork for it. Originally, they were set to be heading back out tomorrow, but it looked like they might just be sticking around for another case.

"It's something that we have been considering. We can move our private detective agency over here. We would get more work here," Sebastian commented.

"Plus, you would get to keep hanging out with all of us," I said, flashing a grin.

The three of them didn't really do social very well. They liked to keep to themselves, but they were good guys and it was nice having them around. They were three more guys who could handle themselves out in the field and that meant I didn't have to go into the field as often.

I *could* work as a field agent, but I preferred to work behind a computer. I didn't like having to shoot people and I really didn't like being shot at. Bullets hurt. I knew that from personal experience and it wasn't an experience I wanted to repeat ever again in my life.

Before anymore could be said, Mason

walked in with Detective West right on his heels. I wasn't expecting to see Detective West again. He had helped with our serial killer case and then we had all gone our separate ways. I figured this case must be one that he had been working on and now he needed some help.

"You all remember Detective West," Mason started. "His twelve year old son, Drew, has been kidnapped. Detective West was on the overnight shift at the station last night. When he arrived home this morning, just after eight, he discovered obvious signs of a struggle and his son was nowhere to be found. He has called his son's friends, but they hadn't heard from him since yesterday. Crime scene has already been called."

I instantly felt bad for the man. Working as a homicide detective was hard enough, but to be doing that *and* raising a twelve year old son... No way was that easy. I had to give him credit, he was doing everything he could to protect his city and the innocent people in it, while trying to be a father. Not many people could handle both lives.

"Have you called his mother?" Max asked.

"No. She walked out of his life six years ago. We haven't heard from her since. There's no boyfriend, either, it's just us," Detective West answered.

Now that was even more impressive. He was working full time as a homicide detective and raising his son *alone*. He was a single father and doing everything he could for his city. That definitely explained the dark bags under his eyes. He wasn't getting the sleep he needed while pulling double duty.

Still, a twelve year old boy getting grabbed from his home, that was risky. His kidnappers either didn't know that Drew was the son of a homicide detective or they did. My money was on them knowing. The kidnapping could have been connected to a case he was currently working.

"Was there a babysitter?" Damien asked.

"No. I didn't leave until ten last night. I made sure all of the windows and doors were locked and the alarm was set. I have an alarm on every window and door, so if someone tried to open them it would go off and I would immediately get an alert on my phone. The security company would be notified and they would notify the police. None of that happened and I *know* I set the alarm."

"If you set the alarm and it didn't go off, then that only leaves two options. Either your son turned the alarm off so he could let someone in, or you were hacked.," I stated.

"Except he couldn't have let anyone in. When the alarm is turned off for any reason, I get a notification on my phone. Nothing has come in."

"Does it still say it's armed?" I asked.

It was sounding more and more like he had been hacked. That would explain why no one had been notified of the break in. It also meant that whoever grabbed his son knew about the alarm system and knew how to hack into it to work around the notifications. This wasn't random. I'd bet my ass this was planned.

Detective West pulled out his phone

and checked before he spoke. "It says it's armed."

"You were hacked. Can I see your phone?" I asked.

He handed the phone over to me and I started to go through it to see if there was any spyware or other backdoor access apps. His Internet usage was all normal and nothing stood out, though. I handed the phone back to him as I spoke.

"Does Drew have a cell phone?"

"He does, but it's still at the house. Along with his school bag."

"How easy is it to hack a security system?" Damien asked me.

"Very easy. Novice hackers can easily do it. I need to plug into the main security hub at the house and then I might be able to find the signature and backtrack it," I answered.

"All of you are going to Detective West's house. Do a full investigation. I have already informed local PD that we are taking over the case. Crime Scene is there on the scene and working it. Don't get in their way, but get what you need," Mason instructed.

We all gave a nod, almost in unison, and started to file out of the room. I quickly went to my office so I could grab the gear that I needed for the security system. With everything that I needed on me, I headed out and started to follow the others to Detective West's house.

I was surprised that Mason was going to allow Detective West to work the case with us, but I could understand why he made that choice. The victim was his son, there was no way, as a detective himself, he was going to let someone else handle the case. It would be better to have him working with us than for him to be out there drudging through the case on his own.

The second we arrived on the scene it was a madhouse of government vehicles. I parked in the first spot that I could find and followed the others inside. The first thing I noted was that the whole place was pretty much trashed and to me that made it pretty clear it was more than one kidnapper. All of that destruction didn't come from one twelve year old boy fighting off a single adult.

Usually, when a kid is kidnapped, there is hardly any destruction because they don't stand a chance against their kidnapper. This kidnapper either had some help, and Drew had a serious fight instinct, or they were looking for something. Maybe they had even added to the destruction to cover something up. I was completely confident the team would discover the answers soon enough.

I turned my attention to the main security hub by the front door. I plugged into it and started to run the diagnostics. I knew in my gut it had been hacked. That would be the only way for someone to get the alarm to not send off the notifications that it was programmed to do. It was also clearly not armed, but it was still registering that it was. There were multiple doors open, so if it was armed the whole house would be echoing with the alarm going off.

"Anything?" Detective West asked.

"I will have to run another, more in depth diagnostic on it with my computer back at my office. But, I can tell you right now, it was definitely hacked. It's still registering as armed and it's not even registering the doors being open. Once I'm back at the office, I'll be able to run some apps to find the hacker's signature and try and track it down, Detective."

"Jonah. You can call me *Jonah*."

"Have you had any cases recently that someone could want payback for?" I asked as I unplugged my device from the main hub.

"No. I've been working homicides. They were all pretty straight forward, to be honest. There's nothing that stands out as unusual at all. I can't see this being connected to me, truthfully, but I can't see this being connected to Drew, either. He's just a twelve year old kid."

It *would* be odd for the motive to be connected to Drew. But at the same time, if it wasn't connected to Jonah, then it had to be connected to Drew or maybe his mother.

"What about his mother? I know you said you haven't spoken to her in six years. But could she be involved in something that could have gotten Drew kidnapped?"

"I don't know. I can't see her being involved in anything that would result in this. But it's been six years, I don't know what she's been doing since."

"We're gonna need to find her. This is too much destruction for it to be a simple kidnapping. You have to see that. I don't know how big Drew is, but he couldn't be muscular enough for a grown adult to not be able to grab him easily. To cause this level of destruction, it's overkill."

"I know. I didn't see it before, but now

that my mind has started to process the events, I can see it. Drew spends all of his time on his computer playing video games. My son isn't athletic. He doesn't have any interest in playing sports or working out. He's a normal and average size twelve year old boy. He doesn't even know how to fight. I've taught him a few self-defense moves, but he doesn't have much interest in it. Whoever it was could have easily grabbed him without making a mess. This really is overkill."

I could see the wheels in his mind turning even as he spoke. He was trying to figure out who could have done this and why. Drew was just a kid, so it wasn't like this was directed toward him. He was just the weapon they were using to cause pain to either Jonah or Drew's mother. We had to figure out which one was the real target of this attack before we would be able to narrow down the potential suspects.

"Well, whoever they were, they didn't want anyone to ever get anything off of this," Max said, holding up a laptop that looked like a hammer was taken to it.

"That's Drew's," Jonah said.

Now that was interesting.

Why obliterate a kid's laptop?

The only reason I could think of was if something was on it that they didn't want anyone to get. I held my hand out and took it as Max spoke.

"Long shot, but can you fix it?"

"Depends on what is broken. If the motherboard is still in good standing, I could repair it long enough to download what I need off of it, but worst case I can just swap the hard drive into another system as long as its not damaged. I'm gonna head back to the office with this. I want to run the diagnostics on the security system and I'll see what I can do about the laptop."

"That thing looks impossible to fix, though," Jonah said.

"I've seen worse," I offered with what I hoped was a comforting smile.

With the laptop tucked under my arm, I headed out and hastily made my way back to the Agency. I needed to get into the system quickly to see what was so important for them to destroy it. People didn't smash a computer like that for the hell of it. They wanted it destroyed and that meant there was a reason for it. I just had to find it.

The second I got back to my office, I set up to start downloading the data from the security system and run the additional diagnostics. I then turned all of my attention to the laptop. I had to take it apart and then I would need to hook it up to my own special equipment that would let me get the data off of the drive even if it was encrypted or partially corrupted. There wasn't much that could stop me finding what I was looking for once I got started. This was the part that I loved about my job.

I had always loved working with computers. I started hacking when I was a young kid, and now, most would call me a hacking genius. There really wasn't anything I couldn't hack. Hell, when I was nineteen, I'd hacked Homeland Security just for the hell of it. I really wanted to know if I could do it, so I did. That success brought Homeland Security

Agent Ronald Evans to my front door.

Evans, now that man was a good man. He had dragged my ass down to the Homeland Security Field Office, but instead of arresting me and sticking me in an interrogation room to face felony charges, he took me around their cyber security division. He showed me some of the cases they were working on; most of them were for counter terrorists. He showed me all of the white hat hackers who worked for Homeland Security. Up until that point, I'd had no idea someone could be a hacker and work for the government. The idea that someone could be a white hat hacker, someone that hacked for the good of the people and not just to commit crimes, blew my mind.

I had fallen in love the moment I stepped foot into that room. Evans had given me a job right then and there. I literally sat down and started working on a case. I instantly fell in love with the entire process. I was able to do a job where I could hack and gather intel, but I could also work on a puzzle that challenged my mind. Each new case was a new brainteaser and I loved every second of it. Evans had taken a lost and lonely boy, one likely headed for a life of crime and disaster, and not only had he given me a family, but a home and a true purpose. He saved my life and I would always be grateful for him.

***

"Yes!" I rejoiced as my program dinged to indicate I'd finally fixed the laptop drive enough to get into it.

It had been three hours since I arrived

back at the Agency and I knew the others would still be at the scene going over everything, talking with the neighbors, and trying to find any security cameras that they could use. I was hoping by the time they came back that I would have something for them.

The diagnostics from the security system had come back, confirming that it had been hacked, but the code was very intricate, far too much for a simple code to hack into the system.

We weren't dealing with a novice, but rather a pro.

The thing was, this pro wasn't a normal pro. Most didn't go out of their way to make a hack harder than it needed to be. The code to get into the security system didn't need to be this intricate, but the hacker had chosen to make it that way.

Almost as if they wanted to show off their skills.

I pulled up the data from the laptop and started to look through the usual places. I hit the Internet web browser history first to see what Drew was into.

"Whoa," I said aloud as I started to see the places he had explored.

They weren't normal websites. Certainly nothing that a typical twelve year old boy would be looking at. These websites were places only a hacker could get into.

Drew had been spending time on the DarkNet.

He was exploring a world that was used by some of the world's most dangerous criminals and any one of them could have kidnapped him if he'd stumbled onto something he wasn't supposed to see. And based on how destroyed the laptop was, that was exactly what had happened. Whoever had kidnapped him wanted to destroy any trace evidence of themselves in Drew's life. It also meant that Drew might already be dead, and if he wasn't, he would be killed the second his kidnappers had what they needed from him.

"Shit."

CHAPTER THREE

Jonah

AFTER WE WRAPPED up at the crime scene at my house, I knew that I would never be able to live in again and feel safe. I knew I would need to sell it and move so both Drew and I would be able to move on from this whole nightmare.

Realistically, I should have probably moved already. This was the house that

Melissa and I bought, the house that Drew had grown up in. It might have been better for him if I had moved us someplace new when he was six. Maybe then it would have been easier for him to accept that his mother wasn't coming back. At the time, though, I was scared it would traumatize him even more. I didn't want him thinking that Melissa couldn't find him when she came to visit. After this whole nightmare, though, we were moving. This house was cursed and it was time for someone else to deal with it.

Back at the Agency now, we immediately headed up to where Cooper's office was. I had never been in his office and I couldn't help but be surprised by how large it was. The first thing that grabbed my attention were the multiple flat screen computer monitors up on the one wall across from his desk, each one scrolling different information. There were computer parts and equipment scattered all over the place and I could tell he used everything in this room. It was clearly designed for him to be able to do anything with a computer and also repair any that were damaged.

I couldn't believe he had been able to repair the damage done to Drew's computer. The thing had looked like it had been run over and then backed up on it. Yet, he had called and said he had something major and we needed to come in right away.

I was hoping he had found something that would lead us to whoever took my son. At the same time, I was confused, because what could there possibly be on Drew's computer that would explain anything that had happened to him? He just used it to play video games and do his homework.

"What do you got, Coop?" Damien asked as he strolled into the room.

"First, the security system was definitely hacked, but it wasn't done by a novice. The code that was used was too sophisticated. It was actually more intricate than it needed to be, telling me this hacker wanted to show off and he wanted people to know he was experienced."

"Why, though? Why give us more than he needed to?" I couldn't help but ask.

"Because hackers can be assholes. Arrogant assholes. They like to show off. They like to hack into systems that they have no business being in just to prove that they can do it. That's not the bigger issue, though. I was able to reconstruct Drew's hard drive and I could see what he's been doing on the laptop. Drew's been hacking into different levels of the web. He's been playing around within the DarkNet."

"I'm sorry, what? No, Drew can't hack. He uses that computer to do his homework and play video games," I instantly retorted. There was no way that Drew could hack. Yes, he was good at math, but he wasn't some computer genius. I would have noticed if he was.

"What is the DarkNet, first of all?" Sebastian asked.

"Think of the Internet like an iceberg. You only see ten percent of it above the water and that ten percent is relatively safe, with the obvious exception of predators. The real stuff is the ninety percent that lives under the water, the parts you can't see. That's called the DarkNet or the DarkWeb. It's where the criminals live. Blackmarket selling, hitmen, child predators, you name it, it's there. But not all of the DarkNet is bad. A lot of novice hackers start out by hacking their way into the DarkNet and then they play around with other hackers. There are video games on there that companies create and get people to play to try and find the flaws within the system. They use hackers as beta testers to improve the games."

"Why hackers?" Max asked.

"Because in order to hack you have to understand computer code, how to write and read it. How it interacts with other codes to create video games. So, when up and coming programmers have a new game they want to test out before taking it to the market, they get hackers to play them and see what bugs there are. They look for ways to improve it. Hackers understand what can be done and they are able to pick up little details that are wrong within the code. The gamer gets to test out a new game for free and the programmer or company gets free feedback on a technical level they couldn't get from the average gamer. It's a win/win situation. Drew has been playing some of those games."

I couldn't believe it. I thought Drew was out of harm's way at home. I thought him having an interest in video games was safe. I didn't care what he did when he was an adult, but I figured if he was so interested in video games, then he would probably want to go to school to be a videogame designer. I'd figured it was best to encourage that and let him do whatever he wanted on the computer. I didn't need him to be a rocket scientist or a lawyer. I just wanted him to be happy with whatever career he chose. But I didn't know he was hacking to get into these games. I didn't know he even knew how to hack.

What kind of parent was I that I didn't know what my kid was doing on the computer?

I was a detective, for fuck's sake.

I should have known.

"How did he even learn?" I couldn't help but ask even as I ran my hand down my face, feeling entirely stupid at that point that I hadn't known what my kid was getting into.

"There's plenty of material out there to

learn how to hack, including YouTube videos on it. If someone really wants to get onto the DarkNet, they'll figure it out," Coop explained.

"Okay, but even if he was playing those kind of video games, that can't be what got him kidnapped," Sebastian said.

"I don't know what got him kidnapped yet, but we can't count out the video games. Sometimes criminals will put in specific codes hidden in one of these type of video games. Hitmen have been known to do it to pass along messages. Black market traffickers as well. They hide their message within the game and the person who is looking for it plays and they see it. Most wouldn't think anything of it, but if Drew stumbled upon one of those messages and went somewhere online that he shouldn't have, it could have gotten him grabbed," I explained.

Great. This was just fucking great. My son was hacking and playing video games on the DarkNet with criminals and hitmen. Clearly, I had been failing miserably in the parenting department. I naively thought he was safe on his computer, but I was completely wrong. I didn't even monitor his online activity. I didn't see the need to invade his privacy like that. Apparently, I should have. Because then maybe, I would have seen what he was doing and I could have put an end to it.

I couldn't stop thinking about how scared he must be. I was also worried not only about his life, but his health, too. He'd had to have a pacemaker put in when he was an infant. We had to be careful with any stress on his heart. It was one of the reasons why he didn't like sports that much. He didn't need medication for it, thankfully, but if he was scared his heart rate would increase and there was no telling what it could do to him.

"Can you find out what he stumbled on or who could have taken him from this?" I asked, waving my hands at the multiple monitors covering the wall.

"It's gonna take time. These guys hide their tracks really well. It has to be hidden enough that not everyone stumbles upon it, but it's there so the person that they need to see it does. It's a fine line that they balance," Cooper answered.

"Is there anything we need to know about Drew. Anything you haven't told us that we could use to try and find who did this?" Damien asked.

"I don't know. I didn't even know he could hack. I thought it was just video games with his friends. He doesn't have a lot of friends, and the ones he does have all live online. He's not a sports kid and with his pacemaker, we have to be careful about strain on his heart."

"Whoa, he has a pacemaker?" Cooper asked, sounding a bit too excited for my liking.

"Yeah, he had to get it when he was a baby to regulate his heart rate."

"You should have started with that," Cooper said as he immediately started to type away at his computer. I couldn't believe how fast he could type. I could barely get out fifty words per minute, but his fingers flew over the keys without him even looking at them.

"Why does that matter?" Max asked,

before I could get the words out.

"Because pacemakers have microchips to make them work. And if it has a microchip, it can bc hacked. I can trace his location from it."

There was no way.

Coop might be able to find Drew from the chip in his pacemaker?

I didn't even think that was possible. I didn't know I had a built in GPS in the kid. I watched as he hacked into my son's pacemaker and I held my breath as I waited to see if he was able to find him. I was praying that he could.

We needed to find my son and then we could figure the rest of this out once we got him back safely. We could figure out who took him and why, and I would sit down with him and discuss the dangers of hacking and the DarkNet. I had no idea how I was even going to have that conversation because I barely understood any of it, but I would figure it out. It was time to man up on my parenting skills.

"Got him," Cooper piped up as a map of the city appeared on one of the computer monitors with a red dot.

I assumed that red dot was my son. "Can you tell if he's okay?" I was terrified of what the answer would be, but I had to ask. I had to know what we were walking into. What *I* was about to walk into.

"The readings show that he's alive. Scared, if his slightly increased heart rate is any indication, but alive. I can't tell if he's hurt, but I don't think he is. The readings are pretty good."

And with those words, I could breathe again. He was alive. My son was alive and appeared to be doing well. And now that we knew where he was, we could go and get him.

"That a warehouse?" Damien asked.

"Yeah. Unfortunately, this just tells me that he's there. I have no way of knowing who else could be in there. I'm going to run any security cameras within the area and see if I can find anything we can use. You guys get geared up and I'll see what I can pull," Cooper said.

"Roger that. I'll let Mason know," Damien said, and spun on his heel, at a fast pace toward the door.

I followed Max and Sebastian out of the room to get my gear on as well. We knew where my son was and we were going to get him. I already knew I was not going to let Drew out of my sight ever again after this.

***

"Okay, so I'm not picking anything up," Cooper said, as we sat in the van outside of the warehouse.

"I find it hard to believe he's in there alone," Max commented.

It would be weird to kidnap a kid and then just leave him alone in a warehouse, but this whole situation was weird. At this point, I just wanted to get my son back and make sure he was okay. That was all I cared about.

"I don't know what to tell you. But I'm not picking up any other heat signatures but his. The pacemaker shows he's in there and it's not like they could have cut it out of him," Cooper pointed out.

"Maybe we're over thinking things. Maybe the kid stumbled upon something and his kidnappers just grabbed him to buy time. Maybe they were worried he would tell his dad. They could be just waiting until whatever they have planned is finished before letting him go," Sebastian stated.

That was possible. He *was* a kid and, unless these were hardened criminals, they might not be able to kill a kid. They could have something planned and they needed to wait it out. It's possible that Drew didn't even realize what he had seen and his kidnappers were just being cautious. It would explain why they had left him alone, why they destroyed my house. They needed to make it seem bigger than it was.

"Either way, we're going in," Damien said as he opened his door.

We all climbed out, but to my surprise Cooper stayed in the van. I figured he might not be a very active field agent with him working the computers. But still, he carried a gun and he was wearing a vest. I figured he would have been joining us. Maybe he didn't go in unless the guys needed backup.

I followed Damien's lead. He seemed to be the one in charge out of the three of them. That was fine with me. I could lead, but I had no problem following either, especially if the person leading knew what they were doing.

Damien and I took the front while Max and Sebastian headed around to the back. With his go ahead, Damien pulled the door back and we stormed into the room. The whole room was empty. I had no idea what type of warehouse this had been, but it wasn't being used any longer.

There, sitting tied to a chair in the

middle of the room, was Drew.

It all felt so weird.

His eyes weren't covered. He was just tied to a metal chair in the middle of the room. He had duct tape over his mouth to keep him from calling out for help.

"It's okay, hang on," I said to him as we worked on clearing the warehouse.

It was empty, though. None of this was making any sense and I suspected that there was more to this than we knew. I had a feeling we were in for one hell of a surprise by the end of it all, because even with Drew now safely back with me, I wasn't about to stop investigating. I was going to get down to the bottom of this whole thing and figure out who had kidnapped my son and why. I knew I couldn't rest until I had those answers.

I put my gun back in its holster as I

went and started to get my son free. "Hang on Kiddo," I said as I pulled the duct tape off his mouth.

"Dad. I'm so sorry," he instantly said, tears welling in his eyes.

I could see that his lip was swollen and there was dried blood on it. I could also see there were a couple of cuts on his arm, from broken glass most likely. It was his blood that had made the blood drops out the door, but thankfully, it was from the cuts and nothing serious.

"It's okay. We're gonna figure this out. I promise, it's okay," I reassured him as I got the rest of the rope off of him.

The second he was free, he was throwing himself into my arms and I was instantly wrapping mine around him. My son was alive and he was safe, back in my arms. Nothing else mattered at that moment. I had my son and he was going to be okay. That was all that mattered. We would figure out the rest, but he was out of harm's way and I could finally breathe again.

CHAPTER FOUR

Cooper

I WAS RELIEVED that we had been able to find Drew, alive and well. I could see the love that Jonah had for him. I could see the deep relief that flooded his body when he was finally able to hold his son in his arms.

I had called for the paramedics to just check Drew over and, thankfully, he was mostly unharmed, minus a few cuts. He was going to be okay, though, and I knew with Jonah looking after him, he would recover from this trauma.

We made our way into the Agency office and I knew we would need to talk to Drew to figure out what had happened and if he saw who had kidnapped him. I knew Jonah was going to want to do it, but I was hoping that he would allow me to speak with Drew first. I had a feeling he might open up more to me than his dad. I would also be able to connect with him and understand what he was talking about better.

Jonah brought Drew into the conference room, but I pulled him and the others away so we could chat for a moment.

"I know you want to talk to him and

ask him about what happened, but I think it would go over better if I did it," I said as I looked Jonah in the eyes.

"That's my son. I'm not going to have someone interrogate him. He's been through enough," he said, instantly in defensive mode.

"I'm not going to interrogate him. We're just going to talk. I know he's your son, but there are things that kids don't tell their parents. He's going to be more open with me and I understand him," I countered gently.

"Coop is right. I'm going to have him run the interview," Mason said, backing me up. When Jonah was about to protest, Mason spoke again, putting an end to it. "This is our investigation, West. You were not officially brought on. I have allowed you to be a part of this *because* he's your son and he was missing. He is now found, and if you would like to see this through, then you have to respect the chain of command. And you have to trust us. Your son is a young hacker and only Cooper knows what it feels like to be in his position. He can understand what Drew has to say. There will come a time for you to talk to Drew about what he's been doing, but that should be between father and son in a place where he feels comfortable. Not at a field office."

I could tell that Jonah wanted to argue, but he also knew better than to press his luck. It would be better for them to have this conversation outside of the field office. In a place where they could both feel comfortable and safe. The very last thing Drew needed right now, was to feel lectured or in trouble. That wasn't going to help us get anywhere. I needed him to be honest so I could try and figure out what he could have stumbled upon.

Jonah nodded, wordlessly backing off.

I headed into the conference room as I spoke. "Hey, Drew, can you come with me for a sec?"

I didn't want to have this conversation in an open conference room. I was going to take him to my office where he could maybe start to feel comfortable in and amongst all the computer equipment.

He simply got up and easily followed me. I suspected he thought he was in trouble, but that was natural. I still remembered how freaked out I was when I first went through Homeland Security. I thought for sure my ass was going to prison that day. That was another reason why I wanted Drew to see my office. I wanted to show him what a white hat hacker could do. That there was a whole other world out there for hackers and they could do what they loved and help people. As silly as it might sound with him only being twelve, he really was at a crossroads. He could either be a white hat hacker or he could be a black hat hacker and I didn't want him to be a criminal. Not if I could potentially stop it.

The second we walked into my office I saw his eyes light up. He was a computer nerd and my office might not be nerd heaven, but it was pretty close.

"Wow, is this your office?" he asked as he took it all in, his gaze flitting around the room rapidly.

"Yeah, it is. Pretty cool, huh? I get to spend all of my time hacking different systems and finding criminals to put away."

"You're a hacker?" he asked, surprise in his features.

I didn't blame him for being shocked. When I was his age, I'd had no idea that a hacker could work for the Government, either. I remembered my own amazement at the revelation when Agent Evans had brought me into the fold.

"I am. I'm called a white hat hacker. White hats are the hackers who use their skills to help people. We work for the government and different agencies, even the military, to help protect people and the country. Black hats are the hackers who look to hurt people and cause general mischief. They steal money, put people at risk, all different kinds of illegal activities. All they care about is the money and the reputation that goes with it."

"I didn't know there was a difference. I thought all hackers were just hackers," Drew said, the awe in his voice evident.

"Yeah, I was like that, too, when I was your age. I grew up in the foster system. I didn't really have parents, but I had this huge hole inside of me that I couldn't seem to fill. One day, when I was nine, I went down to the community center to try and get some of my homework done. There were these three eighteen year olds there and they were hacking. I was really good at math and I was curious as to what they were doing. They started to teach me. It didn't take long before I was able to hack just as well as they could. I'm what is known as a hacking prodigy, apparently. If there's a microchip in it, I can hack it. It's how we found you. I was able to hack your pacemaker and I got your location from it."

"It's hackable? No way!" he squealed as he slid into one of my chairs.

"Yup. If there's a microchip or it's online, it can be hacked. Just like your security system was hacked. You know, hanging out with those hackers at the community center, it started to fill in that hole inside of me. I started to have real friends and I felt like I had something special. The better I got, the more impressed they got, the better I felt. I wanted to be their friend. I wanted them to like me. So, when they asked me to hack different databases, different banking systems, I didn't think twice. I jumped in with both hands." I chuckled at the variation of the typical expression.

"You were a *black hat hacker*?" Drew intoned.

It felt like such a long time ago. I was only twenty-nine, so it wasn't really all that long ago, but I had come such a long way since then.

"At one point in my life I was. I didn't know any better and I didn't want to lose the only people I thought were my friends. When I was nineteen, I decided to hack into Homeland Security. I wanted to see if I could do it. I was bored and decided it might be fun to try. I was able to do it, and then a Homeland Security Agent picked me up within an hour. Only, instead of arresting me, he showed me around their cyber division and I started working for them that same day. That was just over ten years ago now, and I haven't felt more complete in my life since making that decision to use my gift for good instead of bad."

"I want to feel complete," he softly admitted, his eyes downcast.

I suspected he was feeling like I used to. It wasn't Jonah's fault, but his mother was gone, had been for six years. And Jonah worked a lot of hours. As much as he loved his son, and I could see that he did, it didn't change that Drew would have a running tally of all the nights and days he'd spent alone. All of the holidays and birthdays that Jonah would have either missed or got called away from for a case. No matter how much Jonah loved his son, there was always going to be a dead body and another case that took precedence over Drew, unfortunately. It was part of the job and there was no getting away from that, sadly.

"I know your mom left when you were six. It can't be easy not seeing her. It can't be easy to know that your dad is out there chasing after criminals all day and night long. I don't know him all that well, but most cops have been hurt to some extent, which can be really scary for their kids."

"It is," he admitted truthfully. "I know he's a good cop and he always says he'll come home to me, that he's not going to let anyone take him out, but things happen all the time. I read about all of the cops who get killed all the time on the news. Most of the time they don't even see it coming. I just wanted to do something that made *me* feel good. That didn't make me feel so alone. I can't play sports with my pacemaker and I don't even like watching sports. I'm the math geek at school. I don't really have many friends. But online, I can be anyone I want to be."

"I get it. You are just about to start

high school next year and I wish I could say it will get easier, but it won't. People like us don't find our place in the world until after high school. But when you graduate, you'll have this whole world at your fingertips. There is so much out there for you to learn. You will find your place and you will fill that hole, I promise you. Where did you learn how to hack?"

"I was playing a game online and some of the other players were talking about coding and hacking to play games on the DarkNet. I had no idea what that was and I started to talk to them. We started to communicate outside of the game on a hacking forum board. They started to teach me and they sent me some good videos for beginners. I got really good, I knew I was good, and then one day, I dived into the DarkNet and found all of these really cool games. I swear, I didn't do anything crazy. I just played the games. I even made a few bucks helping with the design of a few of them. It was just fun. That's all it was supposed to be. Something to pass the time and keep my mind engaged."

And for the most part, it would be fun. It would be safe for him to be on it and to explore, but he should be doing that with someone experienced who could make sure he didn't fall into any rabbit holes that could get him hurt or kidnapped, like what had just happened to him.

"The DarkNet is made up of a lot of different things. Some of those things are relatively safe, like playing those games. A lot of them are designed by novice game developers or start up companies and they are looking for honest feedback and help with the bugs. There's nothing wrong with that. But the DarkNet is also where dangerous criminals live. And not just hackers. There's black market organ trafficking, human traffickers, gun and drug traffickers, there are hitmen who get their contracts and payments through the DarkNet, and so much more. It's not safe to swim around in it, unless you know where you are going."

"I didn't know that. I thought it was just this hacker playground." Drew said and I could hear the honesty and surprise in his voice.

"And in a way it is, but you have to be careful you don't trip into someone else's sandbox. Which is what I think happened to you. Some of those criminals will hack into those games to leave a message for someone. I think you stumbled onto something, saw something you weren't supposed to, and they grabbed you."

"I didn't see their faces. They wore masks that covered them fully, even their necks, and they wore black, long-sleeved shirts. But there were three of them and the one guy said I shouldn't have gone *there*. I didn't get what he meant, but now maybe I do. Maybe I went somewhere in one of the games that I wasn't supposed to. But if I did, I don't know what it was or what I had supposedly seen. I play a lot of games, everyday. Nothing really stands out."

That's what I was afraid of. I could tell from his browser history that he game-hopped a lot. It was going to take time to figure out what he'd seen and in what game. It wasn't going to be quick and I was going to have to dig into each of the games myself to see if I could find what he might have stumbled across. The trick was, he was still young. His mind wouldn't pick up everything that the games had to offer. So even if he saw something, he wouldn't have thought anything of it. These kidnappers either overreacted, or they were being extremely cautious. And if it was the latter, that meant whatever they were planning was going to be huge.

"That's okay. I'll go into the games and see what I can find. We'll find the guys who grabbed you. And now that we know you are on their radar, we can keep you safe. Come on, let's get you back to your dad and we can figure this all out."

I had no idea what was going to come from this, but I knew we would figure it out. I just hoped we would be able to figure it out before it was too late.

CHAPTER FIVE

Jonah

I HATED NOT being able to be in there with my son. He was *my son*. I should have been able to talk to him and figure out what was going on.

I still couldn't believe it. I couldn't fathom that I'd had no idea he was hacking or going into this DarkNet place. I still didn't understand it all. I wasn't against computers, but I only knew the basics of them. I was a homicide detective. I could check emails and run reports, but I couldn't hack into someone's computer if it was password protected.

I was never very good with math and science in school. I was more of an English person. Drew was the polar opposite of me. He could read, but he didn't love to read. He could do math, though, even from an early age when all of the other kids were learning their numbers, he had already figured out how to add and subtract them. He had always been gifted with numbers. Maybe that was how he learned how to hack. He would have had to learn how to code first, though.

It bothered me a great deal to know

that my own son had this skill that I knew nothing about. I knew I was working a lot and I knew it left him alone often, but I was trying to be there for him. I thought we had good communication between us. I didn't think he was hiding anything from me. I wouldn't have understood most of what he said, but we could have talked about him learning how to code and wanting to explore that more. I certainly would have told him about the dangers of hacking, not to mention the fact that it was illegal. There was no telling what he could have stumbled upon. There was going to be a rather lengthy discussion about it when we got home tonight.

Finally, the door to Cooper's office opened and they both walked out.

"Why don't we grab Mason and meet in

the conference room?" Cooper suggested.

"I'll go grab him," Sebastian said with a nod.

We all made our way to the conference room. I put my arm around Drew so he knew I was there for him. I was on his side. If he wanted to be a hacker, then there were other ways to go about doing it. I knew that law enforcement and different agencies employed hackers to help with evidence collection and to track suspects or victims down. I wasn't against that type of hacking. My issue was that in order to be good at hacking, he'd have to practice it and, as far as I knew, there were only illegal ways available to the general public to practice hacking. I wasn't going to tolerate any illegal activity, especially with him only being twelve. He was too young to be playing in that kind of volatile world and it needed to stop. We all sat down and a moment later Sebastian was back with Mason.

"It's good to see that you are okay, Drew," Mason started as he walked in the room, flashing a warm smile at Drew.

"Thank you, Sir," he said back, slightly awkward given the situation he was in.

"What do we know?" Mason asked, looking to get all of the information that he could.

"Drew has been playing some games on the DarkNet. I believe he stumbled upon something he wasn't supposed to see and that made some people nervous," Cooper started.

"We found him in a warehouse, completely untouched and not guarded. They'd just left him gagged and tied to a chair. We think the destruction at the house was done to throw us off. Whoever grabbed Drew, they didn't want to hurt him or kill him. Everything points to the idea that they have to be planning something that is time sensitive and they just needed to keep him quiet until it was played out," Damien added.

"But I didn't see anything," Drew lightly mumbled, his eyes downcast, but we were all able to hear him.

"And that is exactly what is going to be the problem. Whatever Drew stumbled upon in one of the games, he didn't pick it up. The only way to know what he saw is to play the games that he played and see if I can pick something up that will lead us to whoever kidnapped him and what they are planning," Cooper said.

"But could it still be there?" Mason asked.

"Depends on who they are. They could have pulled it out of the game code by now to protect themselves. It really depends on what the plan is," Cooper answered.

"We're also working against a clock. They didn't want to kill him. They wore masks, so they were going to let him go when this was all over and done with. Which means whatever they are planning, it likely has to be within the next seventy hours or so. A kid goes three days of no water and he's dead. Someone knew what they were doing. Knew he'd been found or escape in time," Max commented.

That was the thing. If they'd grabbed Drew to hold him off from reporting what he saw to anyone, then they had to be acting out their plan soon. If they waited too long they risked not only Drew dying, but him being found before they could put their plan into action. They had to have known I was a cop and if someone kidnaps a cop's son, the entire police force went looking for him on red alert. They had to know the streets would be flooded with cops just trying to find him. But maybe that was the point. Maybe it was more than Drew seeing something.

"What if we're missing something?" I said as I started to put the pieces together.

"We're missing a lot," Max stated.

"I mean about the kidnapping. They grabbed Drew to keep him quiet, I get that and I agree. He must have seen something for them to target him. But they knew where he lived, how to get through my security system. They had to have known I was a detective. And if they knew all of that and are criminals, then they had to have known that if you kidnap the son of a Baton Rouge Detective the entire police force would be out looking for him and running down leads. The streets are going to be flooded with cops working this case," I started to explain.

"Oh," Cooper said with complete understanding as he turned to his computer and started to type away.

"What?" Sebastian asked, confused.

"They have flooded the streets with police, but those police are too busy looking for kidnappers. Which means response times for other crimes are going to go down. They created the perfect window to commit a crime. My guess, a robbery," Mason said as he caught on to my train of thought.

"That's smart. Use a DarkNet game to communicate with your partners. No one within law enforcement would be looking for it; most wouldn't know how to get to the DarkNet. You set it all up and then you kidnap a kid and while everyone is busy looking for that kid, you hit your target," Sebastian said.

"But if this works that means they'll do it again. They could kidnap another kid of a detective to get the same result. They might have already been planning to do that the whole time and the fact that Drew saw something changed who they were going to pick," Max added.

"Drew, what time roughly were you grabbed?" Cooper asked.

"Um, I was asleep, but I think around four in the morning."

Goddammit.

COOPER

He had been kidnapped and I was sitting at my desk at work trying to solve a case. I hated that I hadn't been home last night. If I had, this never would have happened. I would have been able to stop them from getting Drew and I might have been able to injure or kill one. We could have used that evidence to find the rest of the crew before they could kidnap any child. I was gonna have to talk to my boss. I couldn't do nights anymore, not until Drew was older. He was just going to have to accept that. It was too dangerous to leave him home alone. I knew that now.

"How many were there?" Cooper asked.

"Four," Drew answered.

"Okay, between four in the morning and now, there have been fifty-five robberies reported," Cooper started, but Max cut him off.

"It's been like seven hours, what the hell is wrong with this city?"

"It's not all major robberies. A few of them are business owners reporting a robbery for someone not paying their food bill and running out. That happens a few dozen times a day," I supplied. I didn't need to look at the list to know that would be on there.

"He's right. And we are looking for ones where the business owner or employees swear they turned the alarm on. They have an experienced hacker in their group, so they aren't going to be targeting Mom and Pop shops. They want high-end, but something they can slip into a bag easily enough. It could be diamonds or cash. They have connections within the DarkNet so they could easily sell the diamonds. Diamonds would be easier for them to move instead of cash that could have serial numbers reported and flagged," Cooper said as he continued to narrow down the possibilities.

"Diamonds have serial numbers, too," Mason pointed out.

"They do, but only the ones that came into the country legally. If they were conflict diamonds they wouldn't have come through the legal channels and then they wouldn't have the serial number. Just as valuable, though, on the black market," Cooper said.

"Wait, there was a shop in the one game," Drew said, speaking with more confidence now.

All eyes turned to him, but it was Cooper that spoke. "What game?"

"Serial Subway. You're trapped in a subway tunnel and you have to run from a serial killer that is trying to kill you. While you are running, you have to avoid being hit by trains. The goal is to navigate through different subway tunnels and stores to try and find a way to escape and get up to the street level. I've played it a bunch of times to help the developer with the glitches. He was always having glitches because of the graphics. Two days ago, there was a new store, it had a diamond with a crown on it for the store logo. I ran into it thinking it was a new addition. I got to the back of the store and there was this tunnel, so I ran through it and it took me up to the street level."

That had to be it. They must have been able to see that Drew went through the store and they were worried he would tell someone about it. That tunnel must have been their real escape plan. It was pretty smart. They could code their own escape and run it like a drill without the fear of being caught. They must have been watching Drew somehow and were able to find him in real life. How, I had no idea and it bothered me a great deal that someone could easily find him.

"Do you know the street name?" Mason asked.

"No, it didn't show it."

"That's okay, that logo can't be that common in the city," Cooper said as he went back to typing.

"There could be other plans that were in that game or another game," Damien pointed out.

"I agree. Until we have these men in custody, I want Drew in protective custody," Mason ordered.

"We can go to a safe house that the

department has," I easily agreed.

We were not about to go back to the house. Not when they had already proven that they could get into my house with ease. I wasn't going to be putting Drew at risk. We needed these men in jail and then, hopefully, I would be able to sleep better at night knowing that Drew was safe from them.

"Given their hacking capabilities, I would like for you both to stay with Cooper. His house is unhackable and if someone tries, he'll get an alert. Coop, you good with that?" Mason asked.

"Yeah, it's fine with me," he easily agreed without looking away from his computer.

I wasn't too sure I wanted to be staying with Cooper. I could protect myself and my son. However, I was also not going to turn down the opportunity to be in a house where this hacker couldn't hack his way in. If it meant keeping Drew safer, then I was all for it.

"How long will it—" Damien started, but Cooper cut him off.

"Got it."

"Nevermind," Damien said under his breath.

"Jeweler King down on Fifth and Vine. I'll run the company and see if anything stands out. Right now, though, they haven't reported a robbery. But if they got their conflict diamonds stolen from them, they wouldn't be able to report it."

"So how do we know if they did or not?" I asked.

"We go in and look around. Immunity gets us through the door," Damien said simply.

Their immunity would come in handy for the cases that I worked. To be able to walk into anyone's house or business without a search warrant, and have it still it hold up in court, that was amazing. I would have a lot less killers walking the streets if I could have the same thing.

"Cooper, you take Drew and Detective West to your house. Start trying to see if you can find these kidnappers. And if you have to, play some games and see if they are planning something else. Damien, Sebastian, and Max, you hit the store," Mason ordered.

"Copy that," Max said as he stood.

We all started to get up and go our separate ways. I took Drew downstairs to the lobby while we waited for Cooper to grab whatever gear he needed.

"Look, Dad, I'm sorry about all of this,"

Drew started.

"I know you are and I'm not mad. But we do have to have a serious conversation about what you are doing on your laptop. I think what has happened here proves my point about hacking being dangerous, especially in places like the DarkNet."

"I know, but it was just fun. I was just playing some new games, making some new friends. That's all."

And I could understand that, but the problem was his fun was illegal and those new friends could be anyone. It wasn't like he was in a chat room with just teenage boys. He could be communicating with any criminal out there. It was very dangerous. Too dangerous for a twelve year old boy.

"First, the fun you were having was illegal. The DarkNet is filled with criminals and being a hacker is illegal. Only hackers within law enforcement are allowed to hack legally, and that's because they are trained and helping people. I don't know much about hacking, but I know that it's very easy to get caught up in the wrong crowd, regardless of what the crowd is doing. Second of all, the people you have been communicating with could be anyone. They can say they are fifteen, but in reality they are a fifty year old man who likes to play with little boys. You being in the DarkNet is pretty much the same as if you went to a Federal Maximum Prison and wandered around all of the dangerous criminals just for the fun of it. It being online doesn't change the danger factor. It's worse, because you can't *see* if the person on the other side of the screen is lying about who they are."

"So, what? I'm just never supposed to hack again? I like doing it, Dad. I'm good at it, and Cooper is a hacker and look at what he's doing."

"Cooper works for a federal agency that allows him to hack to find victims and criminals. And I have no problem with you doing that type of hacking. If you want to hack to save people lives and put criminals behind bars, then I am all for it. I am against you hacking into a world filled with criminals."

"I have to practice hacking to get better at it. That's what the DarkNet is for."

"The DarkNet is for criminals to hang out without getting caught. I know this is way out of my league. I get that, I do, Son. But we don't know that the DarkNet is the only place you can practice your hacking.

If this is something that you are truly interested in doing, if this is something that you could see yourself doing for the rest of your life, then I will support you, but we have to do it right. We can talk to Cooper. He probably knows how you can get the practice and training that you need without the danger of the DarkNet. I'm not saying don't be a hacker. I am just saying that there is a right and wrong way to learn. The DarkNet is the wrong way, so let's find you the right way."

I wasn't going to order him to never hack again. If that was his passion, if that was what he wanted to do for the rest of his life, if that was his calling, then, I was all for it. I would support him and be there for him, just like I would if he told me he wanted to be a doctor. But we had to do it safely. Just like if he told me he wanted to be a boxer, we had to make sure he was safe while he was learning.

"Okay, I'll ask him. I really do like doing it, Dad. I'm good at it and that makes me feel good about myself. I want to keep learning more about it and maybe work for a government agency one day. I didn't even know hackers could do the things that Cooper does. I didn't know there were black hat and white hat hackers out there. I want to know more."

"Then we can talk to Cooper and learn more about it. But from now on, no more DarkNet. We can't go through that again."

I couldn't go through it again. It was too hard and too much. The thought of losing him, the thought of not knowing where he was or if he was going to be alive when I found him. Nope. No way was I taking any of those chances again.

"I promise. I really didn't think anything like this would happen. It was just supposed to be fun."

I pulled him in for a hug as I spoke. "I love you."

"I love you too, Dad."

I let out a long breath. I had finally found Drew, but that didn't mean he was completely safe. He wouldn't be totally safe until we found his kidnappers. I was just glad that the Agency was still going to be helping me with this case and they were taking Drew's safety seriously. With any luck, we would be able to find these kidnappers and get them behind bars where they belonged. Then, Drew and I could finally start to put this whole mess behind us.

CHAPTER SIX

Cooper

I WAS SURPRISED that Mason wanted them to stay with me, but at the same time it made sense. If these kidnappers decided they needed to get rid of Drew, they wouldn't be able to hack into my house.

That was assuming they could figure out where he was being held. If they were able to follow basic police procedures they would know that he wouldn't be able to go back to his house with it still being a crime scene. Not to mention that the police force wouldn't allow Drew to be without police protection. The kidnappers only had two options, kill him or wait it out until the police moved on to another crime. That was why I thought they were going to kidnap another kid for their next heist.

And there would be another heist. It wouldn't make sense for them to only do this once, especially if it went perfectly. Yes, we found Drew, but chances were they had already done the robbery and were waiting for the right time to release Drew. They were operating in the DarkNet, meaning they would be targeting places that wouldn't want or be able to report the robberies. Places that used conflict diamonds would be perfect for this crew. They could steal them and sell them easily on the black market. Hell, they could sell them to a fence in town that would then unload them. It was a good way to make a quick hundred grand and the businesses wouldn't be able to report the robbery without putting themselves in jail. It was a victimless crime, if you ignored the kid they were kidnapping to make a clean getaway.

Everything within me was telling me this wasn't the first time they had done this, either. They had everything planned and executed without a mistake. They hadn't left any evidence behind that we could use to find them. They wore gloves, long sleeved shirts, and masks. They made sure to be covered up so they didn't leave any fingerprints or DNA. Plus, they covered their whole body so if they did have any scars or tattoos, the kids wouldn't be able to see them. They had thought this through and that could only come from experience. I had no doubt they had done this before and I needed to find their earlier crimes. Hopefully, that might lead us to them.

Pulling up to my house, I parked in my garage and then we all climbed out of my car. I used my phone to unlock my door and we trekked inside.

"You don't have a key?" Drew asked.

"Nope. Locks can be picked. Everything is electronic. It's my own system, so it's not on a circuit anywhere or on the market. There's no research that someone can use to hack into my system. And if anyone tries to hack into my system, I get an alarm and I can counter the attack."

It was a system I had created after I started working for Homeland Security. I had discovered very quickly that my job was dangerous, even though I was behind the scenes. When you were as skilled at hacking as I was, there was always going to be someone looking for me to hack for them. And with killers and deadly criminals out there looking to hurt the person responsible for putting them in jail, it was better to have a proper secured system. It allowed me to be in my home and not have to worry about being hacked or someone breaking in.

"What if someone steals your phone?" Jonah asked.

I got asked that a lot. In theory, if someone stole my phone they would be able to use it to access my home. The trick was, my phone didn't have a normal security system in it like everyone else's phones. I'd made sure to upgrade it with my own software.

"Even if someone stole my phone, it can only be unlocked with my retina scan and my resting heart rate. If they try twice, it will automatically wipe itself and be useless to them."

"Seems like a lot of extra security just to avoid having a key," Jonah commented.

"Yeah, and how did that key work for you?" I countered with a smirk.

"Touche," he said under his breath.

"I have one spare bedroom. It's upstairs, third door on the right. Make yourselves at home," I said as I strode to the living room so I could get set up and started.

"You take the bedroom, Drew. I can crash on the couch."

"Okay."

I could hear Drew going up the stairs as Jonah came into the living room, tossing his bag down on the floor by the chair. I could feel the energy radiating off of him. He was anxious and antsy. He didn't like not being out in the field and chasing down leads, chasing down the bad guys. I had a feeling he was going to be antsy until we caught these guys. He finally sat down on the arm of the chair as I got my gear set up.

"I appreciate you letting us stay here."

"It's no problem. My place is the safest place for Drew to be."

I didn't normally have people over. I wasn't anti-social, but I did like my own space. I liked to live in the virtual world and I often spent my free time on the DarkNet trying to find dangerous killers or pedophiles. There weren't many people who could hack as well as I could and, because of that, I tried to do everything I could to help eliminate criminals. I enjoyed the challenge of it and the reward of knowing that someone dangerous was put behind bars or in the ground, unable to hurt anyone ever again. I looked up as Drew came back down the stairs as he spoke.

"So, what do we do now?"

"*We* don't do anything. The Agency will find your kidnappers and arrest them. *You* need to focus on your school work so you don't fall behind while you are on house arrest."

I could tell that Drew wasn't happy that he was going to be sidelined, but

Jonah was right. He was only twelve, this world was far too dangerous for him to be poking around in. Though, there was something he could do to feel like he was being involved.

"Actually, Drew, do you think you could write me a list of all the games you have played on the DarkNet in the past thirty days. And note any changes that you noticed in them within that time frame? That would help me to try and recreate what you have done and see if there are any new changes that weren't there before."

"Yeah, definitely. I can do that," he said, enthused.

"There was something that we wanted to talk to you about, Cooper," Jonah started.

"All right, what's up?" I asked, giving

them my full attention.

As badly as I wanted to get started on tracking down these guys, I also didn't want to ignore any of their questions or concerns. This type of world was confusing and a lot of the time people got lost in it. I didn't want Drew to get lost in his interest for hacking and I didn't want Jonah to think it was all bad, either, because it wasn't.

"Drew is clearly interested in the hacking world. I told him that he wasn't allowed to be on the DarkNet anymore because of the obvious dangers. However, he is interested in learning more and growing his skills. Is there a way he could do that where it won't attract criminals?"

"Oh, for sure. Homeland Security offers a virtual course for hackers of all levels between twelve and eighteen years of age. They teach kids how to do white hat hacking with simulated cases. They also have camps in the summer for in person learning and to get to meet other hackers around your age. Then, once you are sixteen, and if you are skilled enough, they get you shadowing an analyst, which is what they call their hackers, and you get to help them with real case work. When you turn eighteen, you can go to the academy and you have a job with them right afterward. It's a great program. It allows kids to learn more about hacking without the dangers of them being manipulated by black hat hackers. Plus, Homeland Security gets to have new hackers every year with fresh energy."

It was a terrific program that I often volunteered for. I wished I had known about it when I was a kid because then I wouldn't have gotten into the wrong crowd like I did. At the same time, though, I might not have met Evans and I wouldn't have changed meeting him for the world. He had saved my life in so many ways.

"Really? That sounds awesome," Drew said, a big smile on his face.

"That sounds like a program that I would be happy to live with. Why don't you get the list that Cooper needs and then you can look into it, Drew," Jonah offered with a warm smile.

I could see that Drew was very pleased to hear that his dad would be willing to entertain the possibility of the Homeland Security analyst program. It truly was a great program and it allowed kids to explore their hacking skills without real life dangers. The DarkNet was not a place that any teenager should be playing in, especially one as young as Drew. He could easily be manipulated into doing something illegal and once that happened, it would be hard to get him out of that world.

Drew gave an excited nod as he headed off to get me that list created. I knew it was going to be a long list, but I would just work my way through it and see if I could spot anything that could lead us to their next target.

"It really is a great program. It's also a good way to keep kids that are interested in hacking away from the DarkNet and the criminals that flood it," I said once we were alone.

"I'm not against him learning how to hack, I just want him to be safe while he is learning. I also can't have him doing something illegal. If he were to be arrested, that would follow him for the rest of his life, juvenile or not."

"I volunteer with the program. I think he would really love it. And it lets him meet other people like him. That's the bigger danger when it comes to hacking. You want to connect with people who understand what you do and what you say. Only another hacker understands a hacker. Just like athletes are only understood by another athlete. The problem is hackers live online and underground. They don't hang out with the popular kids or go to school parties. The program can help him with connecting to other people like him. It will help him feel like he's not so alone in the world."

"It sounds like you are speaking from

experience," Jonah said as he finally went and plopped down in the chair.

"I was around his age when I got in with the wrong crowd. Only, I grew up in foster care, so I didn't have any parents to make sure I wasn't doing something illegal. That I wasn't being manipulated and used for someone else's gain. Thankfully, the one time I did get caught as an adult, it was by a very understanding and open-minded Homeland Security Agent who offered me a job instead of sending me to prison. He changed my life and ever since I have been dedicated to helping other young hackers see that they don't have to commit crimes to feel like they belong somewhere."

It wasn't easy. There had been plenty of times even after I joined Homeland

Security that I wanted to reach out to old friends. It took a couple of years before I was able to leave it all behind me, for me to understand that they weren't truly my friends and only using me for my skills, and no longer connect with them. Now, I was in a position to help kids grow their skills in a safe environment with other kids who they would be safe to connect with.

"I'm glad you were able to overcome your past and have been able to use your skills for good. And now, you are helping to put criminals behind bars and keep people safe. You doing that from a computer doesn't make you any less of an Agent or a good cop," Jonah said, flashing me a warm smile.

"Drew will find his place in the world, especially if he has you in his corner. And now he has me, too."

I wasn't about to leave Drew on his own. He needed someone who could teach him what he was capable of. Someone who would be able to show him the right way to hack. I was more than happy to do that. First though, we had to catch the people responsible for his kidnapping and then, he would be able to go back to living his life.

Hopefully, Damien, Sebastian, and Max were able to find something at the jewelry store that we could use to catch these bastards before another kid was kidnapped.

CHAPTER SEVEN

Jonah

IT WAS JUST after eleven at night and when I should have been able to relax and get some sleep, I couldn't get my body to do just that.

Drew had gone off to bed a couple of hours ago. He was exhausted from the trauma of being kidnapped and barely getting much sleep the night before. It was good that he was able to fall asleep, but I was fully prepared for him to have nightmares tonight.

Even though he hadn't been hurt, really, I knew being kidnapped was still a traumatic event. He was going to have nightmares about it, and I knew he wasn't going to feel safe in our home. We were going to have to move to give us a fresh start. I would have to find a place in the same area, though, so he could go to the same school. I didn't want to pull him out in the middle of a school year, not to mention he had friends at his school. He didn't have many friends and I was not about to take him away from the ones that he did have.

I had been worried about Drew at school. I had been worried about him not having that many friends and spending all of his time playing video games. As it turned out, I had a reason to be worried about the time he was spending on his computer playing video games. I didn't think he would be hacking and playing games on the DarkNet, though. Now that I knew about it, we could make sure he went about growing his skill and learning more the right way. I would be looking into this outreach program offered by Homeland Security. It sounded like a more than fair compromise where Drew would be able to learn more, but also be safe, and I wouldn't have to worry about him playing on the DarkNet.

I paced another round of Cooper's living room. I couldn't get myself to calm down. I couldn't get my body to relax. I was feeling antsy. I wanted to be out there looking for the ones responsible for kidnapping my son. I wanted to hunt them down and get justice for my son. Damien, Max, and Sebastian had gone to the jewelry store and were able to confirm that they had been robbed. They didn't report it because, as we expected, they were using conflict diamonds. They had two million in diamonds stolen from them. It was nowhere near the amount they could have gotten from a larger jeweler and we suspected this was just the dry run. They wanted to make sure their plan to kidnap a police officer's kid would work to keep the police response time down.

It didn't matter if the shop owner would report the robbery or not. If you were out on the street and saw four armed men going into a store wearing masks, you would report it to the police.

They had to get in, get the diamonds, and get out before the police would have time to respond. On average, it would take less than five minutes for the police to arrive on scene of an active crime. However, with every cop being out there looking for a cop's kid, that response time could reach fifteen minutes, giving the robbers plenty of time to grab the diamonds and make a clean getaway.

Damien, Max, and Sebastian were working the crime scene. The owner said the thieves were fully covered head-to-toe in clothes, just like Drew had said, so we weren't going to be able to make an ID on them that way. Hopefully, though, there was a camera in the area that we could use to make an ID once they were in the getaway vehicle. They weren't going to be driving the whole way with their faces fully covered. They would have to take the masks off at some point and hopefully, we would be able to get them on camera and run facial recognition.

The shop owner was also not interested in reporting the robbery or filing an official complaint, but we didn't expect him to. Conflict diamonds were cheaper to buy, but they were still illegal. They were responsible for funding the war in Africa and as such, they were made illegal to mine and purchase.

"You are making me dizzy," Cooper said as he glanced up from his laptop.

I had been pacing back and forth all around his living room for close to three hours now. I couldn't help it. I had all of this anxious energy that I needed to work off.

More often than not, when this type of

restless energy crept up on me, I would go for a run, but I wasn't about to leave Drew here alone with someone he hardly knew, even if I was sure deep down that I could trust Cooper. If I didn't feel like going for a run, I would sometimes call one of my fuck buddies up and work it off sexually. That was not a possibility right now, either, because again, I needed to be here with Drew to ensure he was safe.

"Sorry. It feels like my skin is crawling."

"I get it. You don't come across as the type of man who likes to wait around for something to happen. You're more proactive," Cooper said with complete understanding to his voice.

"I can sit for days on a stake out, but it's this part that I hate. Having no leads and waiting around for the criminals to commit another crime. And that is before you factor in that they could be going after another kid of a fellow cop. We're stuck in this waiting period and there isn't anything I can do because I don't play video games."

Our best chance of catching these guys was through the games that they hacked into and set up the code that would lead us to their next target. But I didn't play video games. That was never something that I held much interest in. Not to mention, I didn't understand how it all worked. Cooper understood how the games worked, how the coding worked, etc. To me, it might as well be written in Chinese and unless it was on a Chinese menu, I had no clue what the hell it would say.

"I get it. This isn't exactly a case that

would be right up your alley and there isn't anything you can do right now. I have to play the same games that Drew did to try and see if there are any patterns or anything that could lead us to the crew or their next target. Damien, Max, and Sebastian are running any camera footage in the area, but so far they have nothing. The jewelry store wasn't in a very populated area and the city doesn't have many cameras up within the area. Our best bet of catching these guys is through the DarkNet games."

I knew that, I did, but that didn't mean I was happy about it. I wanted to be more proactive. I wanted to be able to hit the street and make these arrests. I wanted to be able to send my son to school and not have to worry about him being kidnapped. I wanted this over and done with so we could both move on from this traumatizing experience and, hopefully, be able to get back into a normal routine again.

"I know. I'm just not used to not being able to chase down a lead or hit the streets to try and find my perp. They are all online and I can't do anything to help catch them right now."

"I get it. So what do you usually do when you are feeling like this?"

"Usually, I call up one of my fuck buddies and have sex with him, but that isn't an option, obviously," I said with a smirk.

I wasn't sure if Cooper knew I was gay. I was working under the impression that he didn't with me having Drew. Most people assumed I was straight when they found out I had a son. As if that never happens with gay men.

Some of the guys I had been with didn't care. They were good with me having a child. Others, though, they got very weird about it. As if me not being out and open when I was younger was some type of insult to them and the gay community. It never made any sense to me, because plenty of men were in the closet and had children. Plenty of men got a little too drunk one night and made a baby. Me having a child didn't change that I preferred to be with men and was finally out of the closet and very proud of it. If Cooper had an issue with me being gay, then that was his issue and he could get over it.

Cooper closed his laptop as he spoke. "Works for me."

"What works for you?" I asked,

confused.

"Sex. I'm game if you are."

"Wait, what?"

He couldn't be serious. We didn't even know each other. He couldn't be offering to have sex with me just to get me to stop pacing. It wasn't that I was a prude. I'd had one-night stands before, especially in the beginning after I came out of the closet. And Cooper was cute. He had that sexy nerd look going for him. Still, he *couldn't* be serious.

"Sex relaxes you. I enjoy sex and I haven't had it in a year. So, if it gets you to stop pacing and I get an orgasm, I'm all for it." He grinned cheekily.

Okay, he was serious. Still, I wasn't saying no, but I wasn't sure it was a good idea with Drew right upstairs. The very last thing I wanted was for my son to hear me having sex, especially when we were supposed to be looking for the men who kidnapped him.

"Drew—" I started, but Cooper cut me off, already knowing what I was going to say.

"My bedroom is soundproofed. He won't hear us."

"Why is your bedroom soundproofed?" I couldn't help but ask.

"I get loud and I don't believe in denying myself sex if someone is over," Cooper said with a simple shrug.

"I like it a bit rough," I warned.

Cooper stood up as he spoke. "Perfect, I like being tossed around."

This was a terrible idea, but I was not about to look a gift horse in the mouth. If Cooper was in need of sex—and after not having any for a year, he had to be in desperate need—I was not about to pass up on an opportunity to have sex.

I followed him up the stairs to his bedroom and the second the door closed, Cooper was starting to remove his clothes. He had his back to me and I saw the telltale scar on his lower back. I reached out and placed my hand on his back, letting my fingers trace the edges of the scar.

"Bullet and a surgery scar. How does an analyst get shot?"

I would have figured that Cooper would have been safe working in a computer lab. I didn't think he would be in a position to get shot. Instantly, that made me concerned for Drew if he did decide to follow in Cooper's footsteps and work for a Government agency.

"I am trained to be a field agent as

well. I took a bullet protecting an agent who saved my life previously. Evans, he was the one that got me into Homeland Security when he could have just arrested me for hacking and tossed me into a cell. The bullet would have killed him. Instead, we are both alive, and I am missing a kidney, but I would do it all over again. I know scars can be a turn off."

I couldn't help the small huff of a laugh. Maybe scars could be a turn off to some, but I didn't have that issue. It was crazy, though, that he had lost a kidney. I knew people could live a normal life with just one, but if something went wrong with that one kidney, your life could be in serious danger. It made sense now, why he didn't get out of the van when we found Drew. He had to be extra careful to ensure he didn't injure the only kidney he had.

I could have told Cooper that scars didn't bother me, but I figured I could also show him. I pulled my shirt off and I could see the shock and understanding in Cooper's eyes.

"I don't have a problem with scars," I said.

I had plenty of my own. Being an active cop in Baton Rouge led to injuries. I had been shot a couple of times, I'd been stabbed and beaten, broken bones, all of it.

Cooper ran his hand over my scars as he spoke. "Bullet and stab wounds. Either you have been very reckless, or you have the worst luck." He chuckled.

"Maybe a bit of both. I'm an active cop and that can result in injuries," I answered as I moved my hands down to his jeans and started to remove his belt.

He followed suit and I pressed my lips against his as we worked on divesting the other of the rest of their clothes. I didn't care too much for kissing, but I did enjoy a bit of it. Cooper easily allowed me to have control of the kiss and the second our tongues touched, he let out a soft moan. I kept the kiss short, though. I was far more interested in other activities with him. I pulled back and spoke.

"On your knees."

He gave me a playful smirk before he easily got down onto his knees. I could see the shock in his eyes and I knew exactly what he was thinking. I wouldn't call my dick *big*; it was *massive*. That really was the only word to describe it. I had been very blessed in that department. Oral sex with me was an Olympian sport.

My nickname in high school and it had followed me on the force, was Hammer. The guys used to joke about how I could probably kill someone with it.

Cooper ran his tongue along my tip and moaned at the taste of my pre cum hitting his taste buds. I threaded my hand into his hair and started to guide his mouth onto my dick. I knew he wasn't going to be able to take it all, no one had ever been able to take me all. But I was curious to see how far he could go. I would let him set the depth and then I would set the pace.

Bit by bit, I watched as Cooper took more of me into his mouth, but when most people couldn't help but gag, he relaxed his throat and continued until he took me all the way down to my base. I couldn't help but moan at the sight. Not once had anyone been able to deep throat my whole length and it was only turning me on even more.

"Fuck, your throat feels amazing," I moaned as Cooper started to work his way back up my shaft.

Cooper moaned around my dick, sending vibrations all the way down it. I could see that he was hard and his own dick was dripping with precum. It would appear that Cooper really liked to give blowjobs. He most likely had an oral fixation and that was more than fine with me.

I started to lightly thrust my hips, picking up the pace, and Cooper only moaned his appreciation even more. I couldn't get over how glorious his mouth felt. How incredible it felt to be all the way into someone's throat and know that they were getting just as turned on by it. My balls pulled up tight and I felt electricity race up my spine. At this rate, I knew it wouldn't be long before I was coming. I would usually stop, but I wanted to feel his throat swallowing around my dick.

"I'm gonna come right down your throat," I moaned out, giving a slight tug on his hair in a light warning just in case he wasn't on board with that.

Cooper let out a deep groan as he started to suck even harder around my dick and I knew that meant he was good with it.

I snapped my hips forward and gave a deep groan as I came hard down his throat. It had been a few months since I had been with anyone, so I had a lot of cum to offer him and Cooper eagerly swallowed every last drop. I couldn't help but moan and pulse more as I felt his throat working my shaft, milking even more out of me.

I continued to thrust my hips, pressing my cock in and out of his lips, ignoring how sensitive my dick was. I wanted to be fully hard so I could fuck the hell of out him. Cooper hadn't had sex in a year and I was going to make sure tonight was a night he would never forget. Once I was fully hard again, I pulled Cooper's head back as I spoke.

"On the bed with your ass up in the air."

"Yes, Sir." Cooper whimpered. He went to get onto the bed in the position that I wanted, while I went over to the bedside drawer to grab some lube. I had a condom in my wallet that would fit me, but I didn't carry lube around. I opened the drawer and immediately saw the lube, but also a couple of sex toys. I grabbed the lube before quickly grabbing the condom as I spoke.

"Sex toys, huh? Naughty boy."

"I get lonely."

I gave Cooper's ass a slap as I got onto the bed and spoke. "I bet you do. If it's been a year since you've had sex, you must be in desperate need of a real dick by now."

I added some lube to three of my fingers as Cooper spoke. "You have no idea."

I could imagine. I couldn't go a year without sex, that was for sure. I would have gone insane by now. I had a high sex drive and when I wasn't working, I was often trying to hook up with someone. It was a great way to relieve stress, but also to make up for all of the years that I had denied myself what my body was craving.

I inserted two of my fingers at once into his tight hole and right away Cooper began moaning and moving his hips back to get more of my fingers inside of him. I placed my free hand on the back of his neck and put my leg against the left side of his ass to keep him in that position. It would stop him from moving his hips and give me total control over him.

"I'm in control of your pleasure, not you," I said as I started to finger fuck him.

Cooper whimpered at either my words or the roughness, perhaps both. Either way, he was clearly loving this. I quickly stretched him enough so I could add a third finger and then, without delay, I started to search for his sweet spot. I knew I hit it when Cooper let go a loud moan and curled his hands into the comforter. If I had allowed it, he would have been bouncing on my fingers.

I turned my hand and started to rub my middle finger over his prostate at a fast pace. I wanted to make him come without even touching his cock. I wanted to show him just how high the pleasure could be. It didn't take long before Cooper was a moaning and whimpering mess on the bed.

"Please, fuck me," he begged as his legs shook.

I knew I had brought him to the edge and I was keeping him from falling off of it. I was also getting closer to the edge just by listening to his moans. It was time we both got what we wanted.

I quickly pulled my fingers out and slipped on my condom before I lined myself up with his hole and pushed my massive dick inside his hot ass. I had to close my eyes as the pleasure shot all down my spine. Even though I had stretched him, he was still tight and his hole was wonderfully hot. Cooper was panting underneath me as I pushed every last inch of my dick inside of him.

"So big," Cooper panted out, the hitch in his breath telling me he was straining with the intrusion, but his body was craving more and he ground his ass around my dick.

I bent forward, pressing my chest to his back, and whispered into his ear, pushing even deeper inside of him. "I'm going to ruin you for other men. You ready to be craving my dick for the rest of your life?"

"Oh, yes, please," he begged.

I moved back and started to pull out just slightly before I was pushing back in. I went slow at first. I knew he needed time to loosen up and adjust to my size. The second I felt Cooper's ass loosening up, though, I was pounding into him. I made sure to aim for his sweet spot and I knew I hit it when he let out a small scream of pleasure and arched his head back.

"That's it, baby, scream for me," I growled as I picked up my pace.

I looked forward to feeling his ass tightening around me when he came. I anticipated milking him and taking him to heights of greater pleasure than he'd ever experienced before. I was going to make sure Cooper never forgot about this night. I had this odd desire to make sure he would be ruined for other men. That other men's dicks would never bring him the pleasure that mine could. Maybe it was cruel of me, considering we were only doing this for one night, but I couldn't help it. I wanted to make sure that Cooper never forgot about me or about this night for the rest of his life.

I kept my pace fast and hard, making sure to hit his sweet spot dead on with each thrust. I could feel him getting closer, his muscles tightening around my cock now. But I didn't just want to feel it. I wanted to *see* it as he dropped over that edge.

I quickly pulled out and flipped Cooper around so he was on his back. I grabbed him by the knees and lifted his legs up toward his chest, opening him up for me.

Cooper easily held onto his knees and made sure his ass was up in the air.

I hissed as I saw his needy hole spread

open and ready for my dick once again. I moved so I could slam right down into his hole and the second I did, Cooper was screaming from the dead on hit to his prostate.

I could feel his legs trembling and I knew he was going to come soon. My own orgasm was building at a rapid pace. After a few more thrusts, Cooper's walls were tightening around me again and then, he let out a scream as his dick started to pulse.

I growled as I watched his beautiful dick pulse with cum, rope after rope shot out of him as I continued my assault on his sweet spot, milking him for all he had.

With a final thrust, I pushed myself as deep as I could go inside of him, hissing at the white-hot electricity that raced up my spine, and came inside the condom with a long, drawn out groan.

Cooper moaned at the feeling of me pulsing inside of him and it made him come just a bit more. My whole body was tingling and I had a feeling Cooper's was as well. He wore a complete look of bliss on his face and I knew my mission had been accomplished tonight. Once I finished pulsing, I grabbed the edge of the condom and slowly pulled out. By the time I had pulled the condom off, tied it and tossed it into the garbage can beside the nightstand, Cooper was asleep.

CHAPTER EIGHT

Cooper

THE SECOND I began to wake up, I
remembered what happened before I fell
asleep. I couldn't help but moan slightly
at the memory. Not to mention the ache
in certain parts of my body.

Jonah had said he was going to ruin
me for other men and he did not
disappoint. That had been the best sex of

my life and I knew there would never be another man who would ever bring me that level of pleasure. I swear my body was still tingling from last night. I didn't even remember falling asleep. The sex was just *that* good.

I pushed myself up into a sitting position. I made sure to go slow, because I already knew I was sore and I anticipated feeling more of it as I moved. He was the largest man I had ever been with and I was fully prepared to be sore and feeling him inside of me for days to come. I wasn't upset about that part. I did enjoy the feeling, after all.

There was a slight stab of pain that made me cringe a little, but it quickly passed, settling once more in to the pleasurable ache. I climbed out of bed and shuffled my way over to my en suite bathroom. I needed to take a quick shower before I could get dressed and go downstairs and face the music.

I wasn't sure how well this morning would go over. I was no stranger to one-night stands. I'd had my fair share of them. I didn't go out of my way to have them, though. I did prefer to have more of a friends with benefits relationship. Someone who I could enjoy and have fun with, but could also share a coffee in the morning without it being awkward.

This morning with Jonah could either be awkward or comfortable. I wasn't certain which one it would be, and it would all depend on how Jonah reacted to our one-night stand.

I was perfectly comfortable being around him after last night. Sex wasn't something that I shied away from.

However, I knew some guys would find the next morning to be awkward. I was hoping that we could avoid any awkwardness between us this time around. I needed him to be okay with it all, especially if he and Drew were staying at my place for the foreseeable future.

I allowed the hot water to sluice over my body as thoughts of the case flitted through my brain interspersed with memories of last night.

Damn.

I gave my head a shake as I leaned back under the spray and washed my hair. I needed to try and get my head back in the game. Being distracted by thoughts of my time with Jonah wasn't an option right now.

We had four kidnappers out there who could already have their next target within their sights. We needed to grab them up before they tried to snatch another kid to increase their odds of getting away. The part that I didn't understand, though, was how many times they truly believed they could do that and get away with it. Sure, the first heist they might be able to grab a detective's kid and be able to get in and out from their target without much trouble. But that was only the first time. Every time after that, it was going to get harder. Eventually, the kidnappers had to either stop all together or find a new plan. They had to know the police would eventually catch on. Not to mention, even if the officer's kid was found unharmed, that didn't change the fact that the cops would be hunting the city for the kidnappers. They had to have an endgame plan, but I just couldn't see it yet. I couldn't help but feel like it was a player in one of the games. The question was, which one.

I was going to have to play the games again today and see if I could pick anything up. I had been doing that most of the day yesterday and I hadn't seen anything that stood out to me. That was the issue, because whatever message or signal these guys were using to communicate, it was something specific enough for them to notice, but vague enough that others wouldn't. This was also the first time I was playing the games so I didn't know what was different. It would have been helpful if I had played the games before, because then I would have been able to pick up on anything that was different, even if they were subtle differences.

The one person who would be able to tell me what was different was Drew, but I had a feeling Jonah was not going to allow him to play any of the DarkNet games anymore, even if it was to help me track down what I needed to catch the fuckers. I could understand that of course, but it also meant it could take me longer to find anything actionable.

It wasn't a position I wanted to be in, but I knew I might have to talk Jonah into letting Drew help me. I would supervise him and make sure he didn't do anything crazy, but I needed another hacker who could assist me with the games. Drew was here and he had the added bonus of having already played the games. The trick was going to be getting Jonah to give his permission.

I got out of the shower and made quick

work of drying off, brushing my teeth, and pulling on some clothes. A quick look at my clock told me it was just after eight.

I headed downstairs and heard noise coming from my kitchen. I walked in and saw that Jonah was busy cooking up some bacon and eggs.

Could this man be anymore perfect?

I didn't see Drew anywhere, though, and I couldn't help but wonder if he was still sleeping.

"Morning," I said as I made my way over to Jonah where he stood in front of the stove.

"Morning. How did you sleep?" he asked, flashing me a playful smirk.

Good, we weren't going to be doing the awkward dance with each other. I was relieved, because I didn't want things to be awkward between us. We were going to have to work this case and considering we'd already crossed paths on a previous case, Detective West was likely going to be a frequent flier within our cases. It would be easier if we could handle being around each other without feeling like twelve year old boys getting caught making out in a church.

"Amazing. I had a very good workout before I fell asleep," I said, flashing him a grin as I leaned against the countertop.

"Just *very good*? That sounds like an understatement to me."

"Okay, the workout might have been the best workout of my entire life. It might have been so amazing that any other workout is going to pale in comparison." I chuckled.

He gave me a lusty smile as he moved closer to me and softly spoke so we wouldn't be overheard. "I did warn you that I would ruin you for other men." He winked and nudged my hip with his.

"You did warn me. And you definitely made my future sex life very disappointing. But I think you like that part. I think you get pleasure out of knowing that you get these poor guys addicted to your dick, only to leave them completely unsatisfied for the rest of their lives."

Jonah gave me a dark smirk as he went and placed his hands on either side of me, trapping me against the counter top. He closed the distance between our bodies and he spoke into my ear. I could feel his crotch right against mine and just feeling how big he was, even soft, was enough to make me moan slightly.

"Is that what you are? A poor man who

is now addicted to my dick? I'd say you certainly seemed like you enjoyed having it down your throat last night. I could become addicted to you, too. To your mouth and needy hole." He ground his hips against mine as he playfully bit the bottom of my ear, causing a soft moan to escape my lips. "Maybe we could be each other's fixes. You give me what I want and I'll give you what you want."

"Like, um..." I had to get my mind to work. It was not very easy right now, though, because all I could think about was how close his body was to mine. How close his dick was to mine and how all I wanted was to feel it against me once again. "Friends with benefits?"

"Exactly. You down?" he asked as he moved so his mouth was just a breath away from mine.

"Yes," I said, softly.

"Good."

He moved even closer to my mouth, his warm breath tracing across my lips and sending chills over my skin before he was pulling back and moving over to the stove once again.

Asshole.

Apparently Jonah enjoyed teasing, which meant it was going to be a very long day for me.

A long and frustrating day.

The sound of my phone ringing thankfully snapped my mind back to the situation at hand. I pulled my phone out of my pocket and saw that it was Mason. I finger punched the green phone icon.

"Hey, Boss," I said as I answered the phone.

"We have another kidnapping. Officer

Danny Montanna. His fourteen year old daughter was grabbed last night. He works the night shift and he allows her to stay home alone while he is working. Mother is dead. Security system was hacked and the place was destroyed. It's the same MO. Damien is on scene with Sebastian and Max."

Crap, if they had already kidnapped someone else, that meant they were going on a heist today. These guys were moving fast and not allowing for much of a cooling off period. It made sense, though. The longer they waited in between, the greater the chance of them being caught.

"I'll play the games today and see if there is anything different in them that wasn't there last night. I'll try to figure out how they are doing this and see if I can find their next target."

That was only part of what we needed to do, though. We also needed to come at this from a different angle. We couldn't wait around for them to do another heist. We knew they would be going after conflict diamonds. We needed to get out there, be more proactive. It was time the guys hit the streets and started looking into potential targets.

"I'll text you the address. Keep me posted."

"Will do." I ended the call and turned my attention to Jonah. I had to tell him what we had, but now, I was also going to have to have that conversation about Drew. I had hoped to maybe feel him out a bit more and discuss it with him today, but that all changed. We needed Drew to help me with the computer end of things now more than ever.

"What's going on? Jonah asked.

"Officer Danny Montanna's fourteen year old daughter was kidnapped last night. He works the night shift and she is home alone. He came home this morning to the house being destroyed and his alarm hacked. Damien, Sebastian, and Max are on scene. Mason is going to text me the address."

"Fuck, we gotta do something about this. We can't just have them out there kidnapping kids so they can rob someone. If word about this gets out on the street, criminals everywhere will be using their blueprint for their own robberies."

"I know. That's why we need to hit this from all angles. I will keep working the games and DarkNet, you and the guys should be working it from the streets. Run it like any other investigation. I will try and find the hacker and, hopefully, that will lead us to the rest of the crew."

"So, we focus on the rest of the crew and hope it will lead us to the hacker. Makes sense. We both come at this from opposite ends and, hopefully, we'll meet in the middle with some definitive answers. All right, I'll go and start working my sources on the street," he said as he moved the cooked bacon onto a plate before he turned off the stove.

"There is one more thing I want to talk to you about real quick. It's about Drew."

"What about him?" he asked instantly and I could see him getting defensive before I'd even pushed the idea. I was going to have to choose my words carefully.

"Playing these games, trying to see what is different from when he played and now. It's a lot. I know it might not seem like it, but it's a lot of work and it would help if I could have someone else helping me going through them," I started, but Jonah cut me off.

"Absolutely not. Him playing those games is what got him kidnapped."

"I know, but he would be doing it right beside me. He's safe in this house, Jonah. I promise. My system is flawless. He would just be playing the games and he's already spent hours on them. He knows what is the same and what would be different. It will be easier for him to spot any differences, and it might allow me track down the hacker faster."

"I don't want him on the DarkNet. That's not a place for him to be."

"And I understand that completely, I do. And I agree, he shouldn't be on it. But these are extenuating circumstances and he will be with me the whole time. I will make sure he doesn't go anywhere he's not supposed to go. And after this case is wrapped up, he won't ever be on it again, I promise. Jo, we have a crew kidnapping teenagers just so they can steal conflict diamonds. It's only a matter of time before they slip up and accidentally kill one of their captives. We gotta catch them before that happens."

I hoped he would be willing to allow Drew to do this with me. I completely understood why he didn't want Drew on the DarkNet, even if that was just playing a game. It was dangerous, especially if you were smart like Drew was. There was no telling what he could have come across, but that was the point. We needed him to play the games so we could see what he could find. If he found their plan once, then he could find it again.

Jonah let out a sigh before he spoke. "All right, but he doesn't go anywhere but the games. I don't want him talking with anyone or doing anything that could put him in danger."

"I promise. I'll be there the whole time and I will make sure he is safe."

"Okay. I'll go wake him up and then, I'll head out and see what intel I can gather. I don't suppose you happen to have a list of the places that sell conflict diamonds?" He chuckled, dispelling some of his tension in that one breath.

"Not really something people advertise. And I am only assuming they are going after conflict diamonds again. I could be wrong, but they would be easier for them to sell."

They could be going after anything, but conflict diamonds was what they had already gone after and most thieves will steal what they know, especially once they become more comfortable with the burglaries.

"Untraceable, fit in their pockets, and can be sold for a pricey amount. I agree, it makes the most sense to go with. I'll see if there is anyone on the streets who might have an idea of any places that could be the next target. Maybe we'll get lucky."

"I hope so."

The life of a fourteen year old girl depended on us finding her. I hoped that they would leave her alone like they had done with Drew. So far, they weren't killers, and I was really hoping that they would keep to being thieves and not cross that line. The issue was, though, I wasn't entirely confident that they wouldn't become murders if they were pushed into a corner. If one of their captives fought back or escaped, they could be forced to kill them. We had to find them and stop them before they escalated and did something that they couldn't walk back.

CHAPTER NINE

Jonah

I MADE MY way into the bar down on the Southside.

I hoped that I would be able to get some type of intel out of the guys there today. I knew most of the people, almost everyone, who lived on the Southside didn't talk to the police, but I wasn't just another cop.

I worked hard to make sure everyone knew that I would be there if they needed help. That I wouldn't let their dead loved ones go without justice. I always did everything I could to keep my promise to them and, so far, I hadn't let them down. It took time to build that trust, on both ends. I had to be able to trust them with the intel that they had given to me.

It wasn't often when someone would reach out to me, but it had happened. Usually, it happened when Fentanyl hit the streets and they needed my help to get it shut down. Fentanyl was one of those drugs that even the gang leaders didn't want on their streets. It killed their customers and brought a great deal of police presence, reducing the money they could make. Going to talk to a gang leader was not how I had expected to spend my morning, but it was what it was and I knew the chances that the leader or his members could give me some insight was strong.

When I woke up this morning, I'd decided that I wanted to have more than a one-night stand with Cooper. Our time together had invaded my dreams. I dreamed of him all night long, and when I woke up this morning, I was harder than I had ever been. It was like being a teenager again. It took everything in me not to go up those stairs and slide into his ass. I felt like he was invading my entire body. I wanted to touch him. I wanted to hear his moans. I wanted to watch as I milked him again. I thought maybe it was just an after effect of great sex last night, but when I woke up this morning with that need stronger than ever, I knew it had to be more than a single night.

I had originally planned to tease him all day before we would be having sex tonight. I was a fan of teasing. I loved being able to wind my lover up and then watch as he exploded. I wouldn't get to tease him today, unfortunately, but tonight, he was going to be all mine.

I didn't get to taste him last night, either, but I would tonight. I was going to take my time this evening and make him come multiple times. If he thought I ruined him last night, he had no idea what he was in for.

I made my way inside the bar and nodded to the bartender who was cleaning up behind the bar. The place wasn't open to the public, but it was a command center of sorts for the Southside Hustlers. I had been here before, so most of the crew knew me.

I made my way into the back and knocked on the door to the office before I opened it and walked in. Drego was sitting at the table with a couple of his guys. They were busy counting the money that they would need to move into another stash house. They didn't bother with covering it up or trying to give me some bullshit excuse. They knew I didn't care that they were slinging drugs. They knew as long as they didn't get any minors involved or sell to kids, I was good. Drug addicts were going to use if they wanted to. Taking every last gram of drugs off of the street wouldn't stop them from finding something else to use to get their fix. If they kept kids out of it, I had no problem with their business.

Especially the Southside Hustlers.

They did give back to their community. The community center and some youth sport teams were only in existence because they gave money back into the community. They cared about their community. They were gangsters and drug dealers, but they did it because that was the environment that they grew up in. It was all they knew, and even if someone came into power and decided to offer decent paying jobs to low income areas, the gangs would still be there. It would take decades before they were able to eliminate the gangs in the Southside. It was part of the environment and all I could do was try and make it safer for the kids and the people outside of the gangs who had no choice but to live in the area.

"Detective West, kinda early for a visit, don't ya think?" Drego said with a friendly smile.

"Trust me, I would much rather be in bed right now. I got a problem," I said as I grabbed one of the chairs and turned it around, straddling it.

"Don't remember hearing anyone got popped," Drego said.

"It's not a homicide, thankfully. Two days ago, I got home from the night shift and my house had been broken into and my twelve year old son was kidnapped."

"Shit, Drew got grabbed. You need ransom money?" Drego asked, and I could hear the concern in his voice.

I had mentioned Drew a few times to him. He knew about my ex-wife taking off and it disgusted him that a woman could turn their back on their own child. The fact that he would willingly offer up the ransom money, fully prepared for me to never pay it back, only showed the level of respect that we had for each other.

"I appreciate that, but we got him back the same day. It turns out that Drew has been hacking and playing video games on the DarkNet," I started to explain and Beta cut me off.

Beta was one of the worst street names I had ever heard. It all made sense, though, when I saw the inside of his house. He had twenty beta fish all over his house. The man was obsessed with them.

"DarkNet is no place for a kid. He's lucky he didn't get popped between the eyes."

"Oh, he got a long lecture about it. He was playing one of the games when he stumbled upon a robbery crew's heist plan. It was a jewelry store that had conflict diamonds. It's a four man crew, one of which is a hacker. This hacker was able to get into my security system and compromise it. They grabbed him and left him in an old warehouse, unharmed and alone. They then used the distraction of the force looking for Drew to hit the jewelry store. They made off with two million in conflict diamonds."

"Smart plan. While everyone is busy looking for your boy, they can get in and take their sweet ass time. I haven't heard about no robbery, though," Drego said.

"Probably won't. Most people won't file a complaint when their illegal diamonds get stolen. Last night the same crew kidnapped a fourteen year old daughter of another officer. If they follow the same pattern, they will hit another spot with conflict diamonds. I am hoping you might be able to point me in a direction."

They were drug dealers, but I knew lots of different criminals had plenty of different connections. When someone went to jail, there was no telling who their cellmate would be or who would be on their cell block. The guys all talked and connections were made. They could have easily come across a thief or someone in there who could be connected to illegal diamonds. Or even someone with connections to the black market. If we could find out who these guys were selling the diamonds to, we might be able to catch them.

"I ain't got any ties to no illegal diamonds or the black market. I'm strictly drugs. But I do know a guy. He's a stripper," Drego started.

"Not where I thought you would be

going with this. Do we need to have a chat?" I asked, flashing him a friendly smirk.

Drego gave a rich laugh before he spoke. "Naw, man, he's not an exotic stripper. He's a diamond stripper. The man is very good with the delicate process of removing serial numbers off of gems. A lot of major jewelry thieves go to him to get the serial numbers erased before they sell their goods. Now, he might know who has conflict diamonds. If nothing else, he'd know the places that have no problem buying diamonds unmarked. Name's Laser. He's down at one-eighteen Cosway Ave. Tell him I sent you."

"Thanks, man, I appreciate it," I said as I stood up and held my hand out.

He easily took it as he spoke. "No problem. And you tell that boy of yours that the DarkNet ain't no place for a good kid. And if you need someone to scare him straight, you just send him down here and we'll take care of it."

"I appreciate that. I think getting kidnapped has been a very eye opening lesson for him."

"No doubt. Be safe, Detective West," he said with a warm smile.

"You, too. I don't want the next homicide scene I get called on to be yours."

And I meant that. Drego was a good man, despite him being a drug dealer.

I had to give it to him, though, the guy running the Southside Hustlers before him, it was a bloodbath. The man had no problem killing anyone who dared to step foot in their area unless granted permission. There had been constant gang wars happening on these streets. That was until five years ago when Drego had enough of innocent people dying on all sides. He killed his leader and took over.

Ever since, gang on gang violence in the Southside Hustlers had gone down. The other gangs still feud, but the Southside Hustlers were known as more Switzerland than anything else. As long as you stayed away from their people and didn't hurt them, you didn't have to worry about them.

Drego had even helped to mediate feuds between two gangs to get the killing to stop when a war reached its peak. All Drego wanted was for kids to be able to play out in the streets, no matter the time of day or night it was, without the risk of getting shot in the crossfire.

I climbed back into my car and headed off to speak with Laser. Hopefully, he would have something that we could use to find these guys.

***

Just as I pulled up out front of Laser's house my phone went off. I looked at it and saw that it was a number I didn't have saved into my phone.

"Detective West," I said as I answered.

"It's Damien. Cooper said you were out working the streets. Did you get a lead?"

"Sort of. I'm just about to go speak with a guy who removes the serial numbers off diamonds. I'm hoping he might know which shops use conflict diamonds. What about you? Any news on the girl?"

I was hoping we would be able to find

her quickly like we did with Drew. The problem was, we only found Drew that fast because he had a pacemaker. He had something in him that could be hacked so we could get his location. If this girl didn't have anything like that, or some type of smart watch or something, we wouldn't be able to track her.

"Hopefully, your guy can give you something. We have nothing over here. The crime scene was the same as yours. It was a mess; the laptop was destroyed. We have a uniform bringing it to Coop as we speak. Hopefully, he will be able to put it back together and maybe get some intel off of it. The officer's security system was hacked, so no alarms went off. According to her father, she doesn't have any medical conditions and her cell phone was left at the house. She doesn't have a watch or anything that we could use to find her location. We've already searched the warehouse that Drew was left in."

They were being smart. They probably had a whole list of warehouses that were abandoned that they could leave the kid in. And without her wearing anything with a microchip, Cooper couldn't find her. What bothered me was the smashed laptop. Maybe they did it to make it seem like they were after something, but my gut was telling me otherwise. They smashed Drew's laptop so we couldn't get to his browser history and discover he had been playing video games on the DarkNet. So why smash hers?

"What do we know about this girl?" I asked.

"Jessica Montanna, fourteen, goes to Seaway High as a freshman. We've sent uniforms over to speak with her friends at the school. So far, though, nothing has come up. She's a good student, according to the report cards that were up on the fridge. No Juvi record. Her mom is deceased as of three years ago. Officer Montanna has been raising her on his own ever since. He hasn't even dated yet. Said he didn't want to bring another woman into her life until she felt ready."

"What were her grades in Math and English?"

"Seriously?" Damien asked, and I could tell he didn't understand why that would be relevant. It might not be, but I was running on a hunch.

"Humor me."

I could hear him walking before he spoke. "Math she gets all high nineties and in English she's in the upper seventies, low eighties range. Why?"

"From what I have recently discovered, hackers excel in Math, but can be pretty average in English. It's how their mind processes the numbers versus words. Maybe she wasn't targeted just because her dad was working the night shift as a patrol officer. Maybe her laptop was smashed because she saw something that she wasn't supposed to, just like Drew."

It was a long shot, I was fully aware of that fact. However, both Jessica and Drew had this one thing in common. It can't be a coincidence that the second time a law enforcement official's child was abducted and they were both good at math and computers. We would need Coop's diagnostics on her laptop, and hopefully, he could get it to confirm my theory. But at least we had a theory, now.

"You think they were both targeted for their hacking skills. It's possible, but I mean, how many young hackers could there be with parents in the police force?"

That was the question, because if they were targeted, then how were our kidnappers finding them?

My gut was telling me this was connected, that they were targeted, but I had no idea why.

Sure, maybe they could have stumbled upon something, but what would the odds be that two young hackers in the same city would stumble upon a heist?

Plus, they just happened to be the only child of single law enforcement officials. The odds were too high to make this coincidental. It had to be connected and maybe if we could discover that connection, we could find out who their next captive would be.

"I don't know, but I'm not buying that they only learned how to hack using YouTube. I'm sure there are plenty of videos on how to hack on YouTube, but it has to be pretty basic. If it was that easy that anyone could get onto the DarkNet, then criminals wouldn't be using it. I mean, we're not talking about how to hack into a phone or your school's database. The DarkNet is used for hitmen and human traffickers, there's got to be more to it than these kids are learning from YouTube."

"You make a valid point. Seems like you are going to need to talk to your kid and see what else he knows."

"Yeah. I'll let you know if I get something."

"Copy."

I ended the call, but I didn't get out of my car right away. Damien was right, it was starting to seem like Drew had been keeping something from me. He was only twelve, he shouldn't be caught up in anything dangerous. I just couldn't see it. At the same time, though, he had to know more than what he had told us. There was no way these two just happened to get grabbed out of all of the children in the city.

I let out a sigh and rubbed my hand over my face. I was going to have to talk to Drew when I got back. I just prayed that I wasn't going to hate his answers.

I climbed out of the car and made my way toward Laser's place. Hopefully, he would be able to point us in the right direction. We needed something that we could use to pick these guys up. I knocked on the door and a moment later it opened part way.

"What?" a guy said, and I had a feeling this was Laser.

"I'm here to see Laser. Drego sent me." It would be best to skip the part about me being a detective. At least, until I got inside.

The guy stepped back and allowed me to walk inside. The house looked normal, but I knew there was a basement and that would be where he did his work. I didn't need to see it. I wasn't about to arrest this man. I wanted the kidnappers. I didn't care about whatever he was doing with the gems to clean them.

"You got something you need scrubbed?" Laser asked as he moved into the living room. He was a sketchy and skittish type of guy. But I guess in his world it was better to be paranoid than trusting.

"No. I'm Detective West with B.R.P.D. Don't start freaking out, I'm not here for you," I said quickly. I could see him starting to panic the second that I said I was a detective. "I'm looking for a four man robbery crew. They are kidnapping teenagers to keep the cops busy while they go in and rob a jewelry store. They target the ones with conflict diamonds. Drego said you might have an idea of what stores are using conflict diamonds or ones that are open to illegal diamonds."

"I might, but I ain't no snitch."

"Look, I don't care about what setup you have in your basement. I don't care about the unknown amount of money you have in stolen gems in said basement. I don't care about your clients or you, for that matter. However, I could start caring about it all and that's not going to bode well for you. I promise you, a few nights in the county jail and you will snitch on everyone, including your momma. You are not the type of guy who does well in prison. So, tell me what I want to know and I'll leave and you can go right back to your illegal activities."

Some cops would care. In fact, most would. A bust like that could be career making. Myself, though, I cared about preventing kids from being kidnapped. I wanted the kidnappers. What Laser was doing wasn't my department and I didn't care. If he wanted to wash stolen jewelry that was his business, and most of it would be covered under insurance so the victims would be able to get compensated for it. Was it justice, no, but they were still living and that was what mattered.

I could see him thinking about it. He was going to tell me, we both knew it. He was not the type of guy who was hard enough for jail and he knew it.

He got up and strolled off somewhere for a moment before he came back with a list. "That's all I know," he said.

I took the list and saw that there were twenty-three jewelry stores on it. This was going to take a long time. We were going to have to run the owners and investigate to see if they could be the target of this crew. It was, unfortunately, not going to be a quick lead.

"Appreciate it," I said with a nod before I headed out.

I heard the lock being thrown the second the door clicked closed. Laser was going to be looking over his shoulders for weeks after this. Every time someone knocked on the door, he was going to be expecting the police. He would calm down eventually, though, and he might be a nice resource of information for a later case. I got a lot of homicides from home invasions. There was always a chance he might come across some high-end jewelry from one of them.

I climbed back into my car and started to make some calls. We were going to need to run these names and do a surveillance check on these stores. My hope for getting back at a decent hour to speak with Drew was going right out the window. At this rate, I wouldn't be getting back to Cooper's until late. That talk was going to have to wait until tomorrow.

CHAPTER TEN

Cooper

IT WAS NEARING ten o'clock when Jonah finally came back home.

Whoa, not his home, *my* home.

That was weird. I shouldn't think of this as Jonah's home. We'd only known each other for less than five days. I shouldn't be thinking how good he looked walking through my front door. I shouldn't be noticing how easy it was for me to spend the day with Drew. I shouldn't be thinking about how nice it would have been for us all to eat breakfast together. I shouldn't be wondering how it would feel to fall asleep in his arms, to wake up in his arms.

Or better yet, to wake up with his erection pressing against my ass.

I couldn't allow myself to have feelings for him. He didn't come across as someone who was interested in feelings. He had already been married, to a woman. He most likely wouldn't want another serious relationship like that.

Not that I was looking for a serious relationship, either. I had never really been in one and I wasn't sure it was the best idea to get into a relationship with someone in law enforcement. Yes, he would understand why I worked long hours and could be called away at a moment's notice. However, he would also work long hours and be called away at a moment's notice. He was also an active field detective and had the scars to prove it. He was more likely to be killed in the line of duty and I wasn't sure that was something I would be able to handle. He wasn't going to change his job or how he did it. And I would never ask him to do that. Even if we were in love, I could never ask him to change his career. Just like he would never ask me that. What we did for a living, it was special, and it was work that needed to be done. It wasn't something either of us were looking to walk away from. It would be better to leave any emotions out of this and just enjoy the amazing sex.

"Hey, you're back," I said, flashing him a warm smile.

"Yeah, sorry for being so late. I didn't mean to dump Drew on you," he said as he removed his coat and boots.

"You didn't dump him on me. He's not an infant; he's twelve. It's not like he requires a lot of work. We just hung out on the couch working away. We haven't found anything yet. They might not be using those games again and it's not like there is a shortage of games on the DarkNet. What about you?"

Jonah spoke as he leaned against the doorframe that led into my living room. "Well, we have twenty-three possible locations that the crew could hit. And those are just the ones we know about. No one has found Jessica yet, so there's a chance they haven't hit their target yet.

We spoke with the owners of the jewelry stores, but they are all playing stupid and denying any type of illegal activities. We don't have warrants to search them, so all we can do is monitor them. We have unmarked cars at each location. Can't really say we got anywhere today. What about the laptop? Is it a goner?"

That laptop was a lot of work to try and repair. I wasn't certain I would even be able to do it, but I was able to half fix it. They had destroyed it more than Drew's and I didn't think that was an accident. I think the hacker somehow discovered that we were able to grab Drew and he wanted to make sure we couldn't get into it this time around. That told me there was something on the laptop that could lead us to something.

"Sort of. I couldn't fully fix it, not like

Drew's. I do believe that you're right. I think both Jessica and Drew were targeted and it has to do with whatever is on their laptops. Jessica's was destroyed twice as badly as Drew's. They made sure nothing could be recovered. I was able to get into it, but I couldn't get to the browser history. It was most likely double scrubbed so it couldn't even be rebuilt. What I did find, though, was a pretty sophisticated firewall and a large amount of hidden files."

"Hidden files?" he asked, confused.

"Every computer has the option to hide a file. So when you look at your documents or desktop, no one will see that you have it. You have to go through the computer to search for hidden files. I couldn't get into them, but the file was very large. I'm talking just over three gigabytes with something in it."

"She's hiding something, but what?"

"No idea. It could be a shitload of documents or it could be vidcos. For all I know, it could be a video game that she is creating. It doesn't have to be a bad thing, but it is there and with the damage done to the computer, I can't access it."

I wasn't certain what would be in the hidden files. It could have easily been a draft for a video game. That would explain why it was rather large. It also would explain why she was hiding it. She could have been worried about someone looking to steal her idea. It could also explain why she was on the DarkNet, assuming she was. She could easily be an up and coming video games designer. It didn't have to mean something illegal.

"And there is nothing you can do to

Frankenstein it back to life?"

"No. This thing is dead, we were lucky I was able to even get it to turn on once."

"Okay. Were there hidden files on Drew's laptop?"

I could tell he was afraid to ask the question, not that I could blame him. He was clearly thinking that Drew and Jessica were involved in something illegal, something shady, and it got them targeted by this crew. I wasn't getting that from Drew, though. I genuinely didn't think he knew who they were or what was going on.

"I didn't search for any. I can tomorrow. My eyes are too burnt out to keep staring at a screen. For what it's worth, though, I don't think he's involved in anything illegal. I spent all day with him and he genuinely just loves playing the games. When I mentioned Jessica, there was no recognition in his eyes. He doesn't know her. That doesn't mean he doesn't know her online handle, but we don't even know what that is so we can't ask him. He's a good kid. I can't speak for Jessica, but he's a good kid."

Jonah let out a sigh as he tiredly rubbed his hands over his face. I could tell he was stressed and worried. That he had been worried about this all day, not that I could blame him. It couldn't have been a good feeling to wonder if your own son was doing something illegal and could be setting a target on his back. With that said, though, I did think they knew each other, but only online. And that was what we needed to get out of Drew tomorrow. We had to know the full story, because I believed he was holding something back.

Like every teenager, he was only giving us what he thought would answer our questions and get him in less trouble. We needed the whole truth if we were going to solve this case.

"I just don't know what to do about that. As stupid as this is going to sound, I almost would have preferred the whole issue to be about drugs. At least that I would be able to understand and fix. I could end that. But all of this computer stuff, the coding, the hacking, the DarkNet, I can't fix that and I don't understand that world. It's like being dropped in a foreign country where English isn't even their second language and told to figure it out."

"If you asked me a question about football, or any sport for that matter, I couldn't answer it even if my life depended on it. You can't be expected to know everything about every topic out there. You are going to have topics that Drew will be interested in that you won't know about. Just like there are topics he doesn't know that you do. It's not about you being able to talk computers with him, Jonah. It's about you *listening* to him when he does talk. Showing him that you are interested and willing to be there for him."

It meant everything to a kid. I wished I had that growing up. I wished I had someone who would listen to me and allow me to share with them what I thought or felt. I had to keep it all to myself and that led me to the wrong crowd and almost landed me a federal prison. I was all on my own, but Drew wasn't.

"I know you said you grew up in the foster care system, but did you ever have contact with your parents? Or one of your foster parents who listened to you?"

"No. I don't really know who my parents are. I have no memory of them. My foster parents were mostly abusive and neglectful. I bounced around a lot and was ignored. It wasn't until I met Evans did I finally have a home and someone who understood the real me. The hackers that I met at the community center, they understood what we were doing, but they didn't know who I truly was. Evans was the only person who took the time to listen to me. Even when I would go on these long technical rants. He just sat there, smiled, and gave the occasional nod. Drew doesn't need you to understand the words, he just needs to know that you care enough to listen to them."

He gave me a warm smile and I knew I had managed to make him feel better. I was happy that I could help him. I wanted to make him feel better and not feel like he was failing his son, because he wasn't. He had stuck around when his wife left him with a son. He didn't have to be a single father, but he *chose* to be and it was honorable. He shouldn't feel guilty or bad about not understanding everything there was about coding or hacking.

"Well, I can tell you right now that today has not gone how I thought it would."

"And how did you expect for it to go?" I asked with a smirk.

"How about I show you?" he said, flashing me the sexiest smile I had ever seen in my life.

I was instantly getting up and following him upstairs to my bedroom. I had no idea what was going to happen or what his plan was, but I so didn't care. I doubted there was anything that he could do to me that I wouldn't love.

We quickly made our way into my bedroom and the second the door closed his hands were on me, stripping me of my clothes. I turned around so I could remove his clothing as his lips finally touched mine. My whole body felt like it was on fire with just a single touch. No man had ever made me feel this way and I didn't understand what it was about Jonah that could do this to me.

The second we were both naked, he was guiding me back toward the bed. I was all too eager to get onto the bed with him. He pulled back from the kiss as he spoke.

"Lay down, but put your head toward the end of the bed."

Well, that was new, but I was more than willing to do whatever he wanted me to. I quickly scrambled into the position that he wanted.

He grabbed me under my shoulders and moved me so my head was hanging off of the end of the bed and I couldn't help but wonder what he planned to do.

"Open up, I'm gonna fuck your throat."

A moan escaped me the second his words registered in my brain. I had never given a blowjob like that before and I was already hard just thinking about it.

I willingly opened my mouth and he started to slide his massive dick inside of my mouth. He went slow, but unlike before, I felt every glorious inch of him as his dick worked its way across my tongue and down my throat.

The second he was all the way inside of me, he was moving back to lightly fuck my mouth.

"You feel so good, Baby, but how do you taste?" he said, and that was the only warning I had before he bent all the way forward and licked at the tip of my hard and weeping dick. He moaned as he spoke. "Nice and sweet, just how I like it."

A second later, I felt his hot mouth engulfing my dick and it was heaven. He continued to thrust into my mouth, making sure he got all of his cock inside of it, his balls butting up against my nose.

I had never experienced this level of pleasure before from mutual oral. This was better than some of the sex I'd had with other guys. I had no idea where Jonah had learned all of these things, but I couldn't wait to find out what else he would be teaching me.

It didn't take long before I was a moaning mess underneath him. He worked my dick with his mouth like he was an Olympic champion in blow jobs. I was gripping the sheets with both hands just to try and keep my body still. I didn't want to lose the heat of Jonah's mouth or the amazing feeling of him being down my throat. I would have easily done this all night long if it had been possible.

I was getting closer and closer to falling over that cliff, and right before I was about to come, Jonah was pulling his mouth off. I let out a whimper at the loss of his mouth and at the denial of my orgasm. I was seconds away from pure bliss and then it was gone.

"Don't worry, Baby, I'll make you come, but not until I'm buried inside of your tight little ass. I got a drink for you, though," he said as his thrusting picked up to a whole new level.

I vaguely wondered if my throat was going to be sore tomorrow, but that thought quickly vanished. Even if it was sore, I didn't care, because this felt far too good to get him to stop.

I wanted to taste him again. I wanted to feel him inside of my ass and to feel the highest level of pleasure that he would be able to give to me. I knew he would deliver, too, because last night he definitely did not disappoint.

It was a moment later when he snapped his hips forward one last time and came hard down my throat with a groan. I eagerly swallowed everything he had for me, not wasting a single drop. He moaned each time he felt my throat constricting around him, and when he finished pulsing, he went back to lightly thrusting to get fully hard again.

Tonight was going to be the best night of my life.

CHAPTER ELEVEN

Jonah

IT HAD BEEN a long time, years, since I woke up with someone in my arms. I hadn't been planning on falling asleep with Cooper, but after finally coming for the last time, we were both exhausted and had fallen asleep almost instantly.

And I do mean *instantly*.

I was still buried inside of his ass with

him curled up in front of me. The sex last night had been even better than the previous night. Part of that was due to the fact that I didn't have another condom, but with us both being tested regularly and both negative, Cooper was perfectly fine with me not wearing a condom. It had made the sex even better and after I came twice inside of him, and him three times, our bodies had given out on us.

I should be bothered by the fact that he was curled up against me. That I had slept with him. Even with my friends with benefits we never fell asleep afterward. I had always made the point and effort to leave once we were finished. It was a boundary that I enjoyed keeping. At the same time, though, I didn't tend to kiss them, and for whatever reason, I couldn't seem to stop kissing Cooper.

I don't know what it was about him, but he made me want to break all of my rules. He made me want to kiss him and feel his body against mine all night long.

I didn't date. I hadn't dated since I'd built up the courage to leave my wife. I never thought I would ever want to be in a relationship again. I had been tied down to a female for a good majority of my life. And with being gay, it felt like a prison sentence that I was never going to escape. I wasn't ready to date, then. I wanted to play the field and just have fun. I wanted to explore everything I had been missing in my life.

And I did.

Oh how I had explored and enjoyed.

I had been with a lot of guys and each one taught me something new. None of them, though, had ever felt as good as

Cooper did. None had ever made me want to feel them in my arms or kiss them.

Cooper was special.

I wasn't stupid enough to not notice it. Maybe it was time that I finally allowed myself to be open to the idea of dating someone again.

Cooper let out a soft moan and I knew he was waking up. I started to kiss along the back of his neck as he spoke in a gravelly voice.

"Good morning."

"Oh, it's a very good morning," I said with a slight thrust of my hips.

He moaned as he wiggled back against me. "What time is it?"

"It's just after nine."

"Drew is gonna be up, isn't he?"

I gave a light snort to that. "Not likely. He's a twelve year old boy. He'd sleep until noon if we let him."

My son was becoming a teenager. He was just starting to sleep in all day and getting weird about his personal space. I knew soon enough I was going to have to have the sex talk with him, but thankfully, that was not going to be right that moment.

I pressed kisses along Cooper's neck as I spoke. "We have two options. We could get up and get some breakfast. Or, you could play cowboy and ride my dick and then we get breakfast. Which would you prefer?"

I already knew which one he was going to choose and I was very much looking forward to it. So far, I had been doing all of the work and this morning, I was feeling a little lazy. I wanted to lie there and watch, just enjoy the view and the pleasure as he rode me.

"I'll take the second one," he said, and wiggled his hips, grinding his ass back on my hardness.

I pulled out of him so we could move into the right position. I reached over the bed and grabbed my belt from my pants.

Cooper moved so he was straddling my hips, but before he could slide my hard cock back inside of him, I grabbed both of his wrists and tied them behind his back with my belt.

"No touching," I said, flashing him a smirk as I ran my finger along his hard shaft, causing him to hiss and let out a shaky breath.

I lay back and watched as Cooper lifted his hips and started to take my dick into his ass. I knew he was already stretched, I had just pulled out of him, so he didn't have to go slow.

I moaned as I watched as my dick disappeared inside of his hungry hole. The second he had me buried inside of him he didn't even wait before he was moving almost all of the way off before slamming right back down.

Cooper let out a whimper as the position made my cockhead hit his prostate dead on, just like I knew it would. He was instantly doing it again, and again. Rapidly thrusting his ass over my cock, moaning and whimpering, more and more precum leaking from his slit to dribble down his hardness each time he pressed downward.

I moaned at the sight of him using my body to pleasure himself. "That's it, Baby, use my dick. I want to watch as you make yourself come."

I ran my hand over Cooper's dick, causing him to moan deeply. I collected some of his precum that was dripping off of his tip with my finger and then brought it up to my lips, flicking out my tongue and tasting his essence.

I moaned my appreciation as his flavor burst across my taste buds and Cooper returned the moan at the sight of my digit disappearing into my mouth.

"You taste so sweet, perfect for breakfast." I gathered more precum from his tip, but this time I brought it up to his lips.

Without saying anything, Cooper parted his lips and, with his gaze locked on mine, he easily sucked my finger into his hot mouth.

I moaned deeply, panting heavily as I watched as he licked his own precum right off of my finger.

He was so sexy, so perfect.

Cooper started to move faster and I knew he was chasing his own orgasm. It wasn't easy for him, though, because he didn't have any friction on his dick. I had tied his hands back so he couldn't touch himself. I knew the desire to touch his dick would be too great for him and that wasn't what I wanted. I moved my hand to his cock once more, gripping him tightly in my fist, and slowly started to jerk him off.

"Do you want to come?" I teased.

"Yes, fuck, feels so good," he moaned as he picked up his pace once again.

"So then come. I'm not stopping you. Come for me while you fuck yourself on my dick. You better come soon, though, because if I come first, then you'll have to wait until next time we're together," I said as I stopped jerking him off, causing Cooper to let out a whine at the loss of friction.

I loved teasing and I loved knowing that I could make this man go insane with the need to come. I was torn between hoping he would come and not. I would have loved to have been able to keep teasing him all day.

Cooper started to bounce even harder and faster. I knew he would be close to coming soon. I could see the precum running out of him. He was going to milk himself on my dick and it was going to be magnificent to watch as he spilled over that cliff.

It was a few moments later when Cooper gave a soft scream as he came hard, his cum pouring out of his slit in long, white ropes, splashing on his belly and over my chest.

I grasped his hips and started to brutally thrust up into him. He let out another scream as the angle made my cock constantly rub over his sweet spot, milking out even more cum from him. The tightening of his muscles around my dick became too great and forced me over the edge. I snapped my hips up hard once more and emptied everything I had inside of him with a deep, throaty groan.

We were both breathing heavily and I could feel his legs trembling slightly from the workout. Now, I really needed to feed him breakfast. That had been amazing, though.

Once again, *he* was amazing.

I had said I wanted him to become addicted to me, but I knew I was already addicted to him. I didn't think I would ever get tired of being around him, of being inside of him. It was like he was heroin and I could never get enough of it.

"You made a mess. Now, you have to clean it up," I said as I lifted him off of my dick.

Cooper instantly knew what I was talking about, and without any hesitation, he bent forward and ran his tongue up my stomach, collecting his cum. He continued to lick it all up and the sight of it almost had me fully hard again.

Once every drop of the cum was cleaned from my belly and chest, I grasped his hips again and flipped him around so he was up on his knees, bent over, face down, ass in the air.

I spread his ass cheeks and ran the flat of my tongue over his engorged, leaking hole. He gave a shaky moan at the contact of my tongue across his highly sensitive entrance. I didn't care, though. I loved this part.

I knew most guys might be bothered by it, but there was just something about the taste of my own cum from my lover's sweet hole that I enjoyed. I also loved how sensitive the guy was after sex and I wanted to build Cooper back up, only to leave him when he needed more.

"Fuck, Jo," Cooper hissed, moaning his appreciation of my efforts as he pushed back to get my tongue to go further inside of him.

I was all too happy to push my tongue into his needy, soaked hole. I continued to eat him out until I knew he was rock hard and on the edge once more. When his balls pulled up tight, and I knew he was getting too close, I pulled back and gave his ass a light slap before reaching over to untie his wrists.

"We need to get to work. We can't spend all day in bed."

He gave a whimper and I couldn't help but chuckle lightly. I knew at this point he was in desperate need for more, but he would have to wait until tonight. For now, we had to get ready for work and get some real food into us. But after we finally did find these kidnappers, we would be spending an entire day, or weekend for that matter, in bed.

CHAPTER TWELVE

Cooper

"I TAKE IT you're a breakfast guy," I remarked as I sat down at my ridiculously small kitchen table, watching as Jonah stirred together the ingredients for pancakes.

"Most important meal of the day. Plus with Drew, I have a habit of cooking him something. Often, especially since he's been older, I have been working nights so I make sure I cook him a real breakfast to make up for me not being there at night. I know he's just sleeping, but still, if he had a nightmare or was sick, I wouldn't be there for him. I know it's not much, but I feel better knowing that I am at least sending him to school with something real in his stomach."

"It's nice that you make him breakfast. Most of the foster homes I was in, it was either cereal or no food in the morning. Those moments that you can spend with him and get to talk and catch up, they're important, even if they are only for a few minutes at a time."

He was a good dad and I hated that he always seemed to be second guessing himself. I could understand it. He was a single dad working a full-time job and, as a police detective, his job wasn't exactly nine to five. He could be called away anytime outside of his shift. He could have to work past his shift and on holidays and birthdays. There were no guarantees in his line of work, but he had taken that on when he signed up to be a police officer.

The problem was, Drew didn't sign up. The kid was enlisted to the life and it could be very hard on a child, especially as he got older. Drew was twelve now, he understood that his dad could be hurt. He would have seen him hurt over the years with those scars. It would be natural for Drew to be scared and pull away as he got older. It was something that Jonah would need to keep a very close eye on to ensure that Drew didn't go down the wrong path.

I would also be keeping an eye on him.

Even once this case was over, I would be making a point of regularly seeing Drew and helping him with his skills. I would be making sure he knew that he had someone in his corner, even when his dad couldn't be there.

"I try. I thought as he got older it would be easier, but now I'm starting to think it's going to be harder."

"Have you talked to him about the dangers of your job and what will happen to him if you die in the line of duty?" I knew it wasn't an easy conversation to have with anyone, but I couldn't help but wonder if Drew was worried about where he would go should the worst ever happen.

Jonah let out a sigh before he spoke. "No, and I know I should have that conversation with him. He's old enough to understand that my job is dangerous. He's seen me hurt, shot, and we've worked through it and I have always downplayed it a bit. The problem is, I don't really know where he would go. His mother wants nothing to do with him, hasn't had any contact with him for five years. I have no siblings, and my parents are older and on a fixed income. They wouldn't be able to afford to raise him if should I die tomorrow. I don't know."

I could hear the deep feeling of conflict and pain in his voice at not being able to have that answer. I could understand fully that he was apprehensive about sending Drew to his parents. I'd had a couple of older foster parents and it wasn't a good situation. They barely had enough money for food and they were sick a lot. Taking on a child, it wasn't easy.

And it sounded like Drew's own mother wasn't even a possible option. Even if she could be found, she had abandoned Drew five years ago. The woman had made the incomprehensible choice to no longer be a mother. Without a relative, Drew would be placed in the foster care system and that was the last thing that either of us wanted.

I figured it had to be taking a toll on both of them. Every time Jonah went out for work, the "what ifs" had to weigh on his mind and that could make him distracted in the field. It wasn't a good position to be in.

"He can stay with me." The words were tumbling out of my mouth before I even registered that I was saying them.

Jonah instantly turned around and gave me a confused and shocked look, not that I could blame him. I was fairly certain I had the same look on my face.

Was I a kid person?

Not so much. I was a teenager person, sure, but younger children, I didn't tend to be around them. Not since I had aged out of the foster system. I never wanted to have children of my own or someone else's. It was a direct result of having to care for so many different children in my life.

Once I was thirteen, I started to become one of the oldest foster kids in all of the homes I had been placed in. The older kids, their job was to help take care of the younger children. When I was fourteen, for six months I had to share a room with a newborn who was addicted to heroin. I spent six months out of school and stuck twenty-four hours a day, seven days a week with this crying baby. I never wanted to have children, not after that.

Drew wasn't an infant, though. He was a twelve year old boy and he might never have to be placed with anyone if Jonah didn't die. However, just the thought of Drew having to go into the foster system, it made my stomach turn into knots. There was no telling what could happen to him and I didn't want him to experience any trauma or abuse. I didn't want him to get caught up in the wrong crowd and become a black hat hacker, either. He didn't deserve it.

"What?" Jonah finally managed to ask.

"Yeah, I didn't expect that either." I took a moment to collect my thoughts before I spoke again. "Look, I am not a child person. I had to raise a shit load of them during the last five years I was in the system. I'm a cat person. But, I also know what happens to kids in the system and I don't want that for Drew. He's too good of a kid. He's too talented to end up being abused and used by criminals. So, if you don't have anyone else, you can leave him with me should the worst happen. I know you don't know me all that well, but he would be safe with me. You wouldn't have to worry about him being abused or neglected. I suck at cooking, so I can't promise anything in that department, but he would be safe."

He gave me a warm smile and I could see he appreciated the offer. I was hoping we would never have to enact it, that he wouldn't die before Drew was an adult, but I also knew there was no telling what could happen in the line of duty.

"Thank you. I can't tell you how much

I appreciate that. I don't plan on kicking the bucket anytime soon, though, so you shouldn't have to worry," he said, flashing me another warm smile.

"It would be great if you didn't die anytime soon. Not just for Drew, but for my sex life," I said, smirking.

He let out a rich laugh as he turned back around to get the pancakes off of the stove. We both heard the bedroom door opening upstairs and I knew Drew was awake.

Aa few minutes later, when we were all sitting around the table eating, Drew asked, "Did you find Jessica?".

"Not yet. We're still looking for her. I have to go back out shortly and help with the search. There is something I need to talk to you about, though," Jonah answered with a quick glance in my direction.

"What is it?"

"I know Coop showed you a photo of her yesterday and you didn't recognize her. However, the odds of you both not knowing each other are pretty slim. Coop, wasn't able to repair her laptop enough to get into the browser history, but we are operating on the assumption she was a hacker as well. That you both were targeted for a specific reason."

"But I've never seen her. I have no idea who she is. And what could we have done to be targeted?" Drew asked instantly, and I could hear that he was getting defensive.

"No one is saying you are lying about knowing her. But maybe you do know her by her hacker name. When you play the games, have you ever talked to anyone?" I piped up, trying to calm Drew down.

"Not in the games, no."

"But you have somewhere else?" Jonah asked.

"On comments for YouTube videos, sure."

"Nope, try again. I know you said you learned from YouTube videos, but I don't believe that is how you discovered how to get onto the DarkNet. If it was that easy, criminals wouldn't be using it. Someone had to teach you," Jonah said.

"You're not in trouble, Drew. But your dad is right. YouTube didn't show you how to get into the DarkNet. And it didn't show you how to hack like you have managed to do. Hackers talk to each other, they offer tips and help beginners get onto the map. I had it in person, but now everything is done online. We need the truth. Jessica needs the truth."

"Full immunity, right here, right now. It doesn't matter what you tell us, you won't be in trouble. This is very serious, Drew. I need the truth before someone loses their life," Jonah added.

Drew let out a soft sigh before he started to explain. "I was watching a YouTube video about basic hacking, pretty simple code work. And it was just for me to learn more about coding and how to design an app. I thought it might be cool to try and create a new app for a game. At the end of the video, there was a link to a free coding workshop. I was curious, so I clicked it, and it was completely free, so I enrolled. I learned all about coding, but halfway through, it turned into hacking. I did the exam at the end and got perfect. The next morning, I got an email from them with another offer for a free hacking workshop. I took it and it connected me with a hidden chat room where the students could all talk with each other. No real names were given. It was one of the rules. You had to always go by your code name and never reveal anything personal about yourself. We were told the owner of the workshop would monitor the chat room and if we broke the privacy rule, we could be kicked out. That part of being a hacker was anonymity."

That was what we had been missing. I needed that link and I needed to get into that workshop. I was willing to bet every dollar I had that our hacker was running that group. Jessica would have been a student and there was no telling who else could be.

"Do you still have access to the chat room?" I asked before Jonah even had the chance.

"I don't know. I can try, though."

"Do you know if that video is still up for the first workshop you went to?" I asked next.

"I think so, yeah. I can show it to you."

"What are you thinking?" Jonah asked me.

"I think our hacker is running it. Black hat hackers, they like to do things alone, but they also like to work in groups. Hackers can be very creative, and when they work together in a group, they can accomplish more. They can build something pretty amazing. Unfortunately, sometimes those things are not a new video game or a security system. It sounds like our hacker is looking to recruit the next generation of hackers. People he can easily manipulate."

"Kids who don't fit into normal school society. The kids who aren't popular. Maybe the nerds who get bullied. The ones who are ignored. They are vulnerable to being manipulated with the promise of fitting in and having a place where they belong," Jonah said, clearly understanding.

"I'm sorry, Dad."

"You don't have anything to be sorry for. High school is hard for everyone who doesn't fit in with the athletes or the popular kids. You're a smart guy who just happens to have an interest and skill when it comes to computers. I know you don't fit in perfectly right now, but after high school you will. And with this outreach program, you will find kids like you, who enjoy the same things you do, who you can connect with. Guys like this hacker, they know what they are doing and they know how to prey on someone. It's not your fault that you didn't see that. You're not old enough to see it."

"He's right, Drew. You didn't do anything wrong. You discovered something you were interested in and had a natural talent for. It's only logical that you would want to explore that more. I do need to know, though, if there are any hidden files on your computer," I asked.

"No, why would I?" he asked, confused.

"You know what hidden files are?" I asked first.

"Yeah, it's where you make a file or document hidden on your computer so it can't be found on a surface scrub. I mean, everyone knows that," he quipped with a small smirk and an eyeroll.

I couldn't help, but look over at Jonah with a big smile on my face. He simply rolled his eyes at us before I turned back to Drew.

"Jessica had a massive, three gigabyte hidden file on her laptop. The hard drive is too damaged for me to open it. But it's a massive file and clearly not documents. Do you have any idea what it could be?"

"Maybe. At the end of the workshop, the runner connected six of us for a private conversation. He said he was so impressed with all of our skills, he wanted us to work on a different project. That if we did really well, we could be hired in his company to work for cyber security and major corporations, backtracking hacks and preventing a cyber attack on their system. We were all for it. I mean, it was a huge opportunity. Completing this project had to be done together. If one of us didn't do our part, the whole project would fall apart."

"And what was it that he wanted you to do?" Jonah asked.

"My part of the project was to create an algorithm that could mutate within different databases. He wanted us to create a skeleton key, but he swore it would never be used. That it was only for a simulation to prove that our key would actually work. It was never supposed to be used in real life. It was just supposed to be some virtual thing that couldn't actually work in real practice."

"Shit," I immediately said.

"Hold up, what's a skeleton key?" Jonah asked me.

"It's like a key to the city, only that city

is the world. It's a virtual key that, when created properly, can be used to unlock anything and everything. And I do mean *everything*. You download it onto a USB drive and you can take it with you to access anything that has a USB port. It's a series of complex codes and algorithms that, when they work properly, can unlock anything with a microchip. I'm talking about online banks, the stock market, power, water, gas, cell phones, anything connected to the Internet. Military bases, nuclear missiles, hospital equipment, everything nowadays is connected to the internet, and anything that is still controlled from an offline circuit, you can use the USB to get in. All you have to do is plug it into a hub at that facility. And it works anywhere in the world. Some guy could be sitting in his mother's basement and start World War Three with a few keystrokes."

This was a nightmare, a complete clusterfuck nightmare.

If this hacker was able to create a skeleton key, there was no telling the damage that he could do to the country; to the world. We had to find him and make sure any traces of a skeleton key were wiped out.

"And you made one?" Jonah asked Drew, now feeling the urgency and the panic.

"No, I swear I didn't. I don't know, it just felt off. I knew it was only supposed to be in a virtual simulation, but it still didn't feel right to make something like that. To help create something that should never be made. I left the group. I left the workshop and went back to playing video games. That was about two months ago. But if Jessica has a large hidden file, it's possible she was one of the other five hackers and that she did do her part."

"It seems like the most likely scenario. He would have easily been able to hack into your IP to see where you were located. The other four might be local or they could be close by. If Jessica did her part, which I think it's safe to assume she did, it's possible the other four did theirs as well. But without your algorithm, the skeleton key is useless," I said.

"But if he has five out of six parts, why can't he just finish it himself? If he's this powerful hacker, why does he even need kids to do it?" Jonah asked.

"There's different skill levels for hackers, but also specialties. Not every hacker can create a complex mathematical algorithm that has the ability to mutate. It's a serious skill and it is something that you are born able to do or not. You have to be a math genius. Our hacker probably can't do it and has probably tried to finish it, but if the algorithm is even one number off, it all falls apart," I explained.

"And you can do this?" Jonah asked Drew, clearly impressed.

"Yeah. I don't know why or how, but I get numbers and the puzzle of it all. I like the challenge."

"Me, too. It's my specialty as well. And there are not many of us out there who can do it. Which is going to be a problem, because this hacker wants the skeleton key, and if he can't find someone else who can finish it, they could come for Drew. I suspect that is why you were grabbed first. They were probably going to come back for you and try to get you to finish the skeleton key."

"Why leave him alone in a warehouse if they need him to finish it, then?"

"Because I don't think the kidnappers know what is going on. We've been operating under the assumption that the hacker is one of the kidnappers, but I don't think he is. I don't even think he's even in the city. He could be in another country, for all we know. I think he's using the kidnappers as a distraction."

"They were probably told to bring Drew somewhere after the heist, but we got to him first. The hacker probably didn't know he had a pacemaker and we could track him. The kidnappers get to be paid in conflict diamonds and he gets to finish the skeleton key," Jonah said, nodding. I could practically see the wheels turning in his mind as everything clicked into place.

"But why take Jessica? If she did her part, why grab her?" Drew asked, confused.

"Maybe they didn't. She did finish her part, that's the only logical explanation for the hidden files. Maybe she left willingly and is going to meet up with the hacker or the others. If the hacker still promises them all work, for doing their part, he could be building an army that could break through any cyber wall. He's not just going to stop with a skeleton key. Even having it, he would need more hackers to help him go through all of the layers of security. And to keep modifying the key on the fly as the Government works to redesign their cyber systems to prevent the key from getting in.”

“So it’s something that he would need ongoing help with. If he’s planning on keeping the young hackers, it makes sense that he has them being kidnapped. If they run away, they would still be looked for, but it opens them up to questioning about why they ran away. If they are kidnapped, it explains why they have been gone and they have an honest reason as to what happened to them without divulging the hacking ring,” Jonah said.

“But why would she agree to any of this?” Drew asked.

“We might not know that answer until we can talk to Jessica. But I have a feeling our hacker has been seducing her. I would be willing to bet that she is the only female hacker who moved on. Her mom died a few years ago. She's an only child, dad is working as a cop. He's probably working extra hours to start saving for her college tuition. She's probably not popular in school, feels like she doesn't belong anywhere, has no one to talk to. Then, this man starts paying attention to her, telling her all the things she needs to hear to feel good about herself. He has probably given her private one-on-one lessons, bought her stuff. She probably figures they are going to be together and right the wrongs of the world. She has no idea that he's just using her, that he's a predator and she's just his latest prey."

"We gotta find this hacker and shut him down before he keeps doing this," Jonah said with a great deal of determination in his voice.

"Assuming we can. I'll work with Drew today to find the other four within the group. I'll also see what I can dig up on Jessica. You gotta find Jessica. She could be the one to give us the kidnappers and the hacker."

"Do we need to warn someone about this skeleton key?" Jonah asked.

"They don't have the algorithm. If they did, we would be reading about it. I'll inform Mason and he can run with it through the proper channels."

"Is Drew going to be in trouble for any of this?" Jonah asked, worried about how this could turn out for his son.

"No, he'll be fine. He's just a kid doing a workshop. He didn't do anything illegal and he didn't make the algorithm. He had a bad feeling and he got out. He's not going to be in trouble for it."

I would make sure that Drew was protected if anyone wanted to give him crap over his involvement. He had no idea that the hacker was running the workshop for ways to recruit new hackers for his evil plan. Most of the young hackers probably didn't even know the true reason behind this hacker's motive.

"I'm sorry about all of this, Dad," Drew said, his eyes downcast, and we both could tell he was feeling guilty, but he didn't have any reason to be. He had no idea that this would happen.

"You don't have to apologize for what is happening. You didn't know that this hacker would try something like this. And if you hadn't said *no* to your part, we might never have known about this skeleton key until it was too late. Now, we have a chance to stop him. You did the right thing and I am proud of you," Jonah said, flashing his son a warm smile.

Thankfully, Drew had walked away from the online threat from this hacker. Because if he hadn't, if he had gone along with the narrative and belief that the skeleton key was just part of a virtual simulation, things could have been really bad. There was no telling the level of damage that this hacker could have done before he was found and stopped. Now, we had to find him and Jessica, more than ever. Hopefully, Jonah could find Jessica and I would be able to find the other hackers and make sure they hadn't been grabbed either.

It looked like it was going to be another long day. Hopefully, at the end of it, though, I would get to have my reward with Jonah in my bedroom.

CHAPTER THIRTEEN

Jonah

THIS CASE WAS never going to end.

We had spent all day trying to find Jessica, but so far we hadn't been able to locate her. I knew her father was losing his mind. Everyone in the department knew that Drew had been found within hours of our search. They had all expected to find Jessica within the same amount of time.

Only, Jessica didn't want to be found.

It was not going to go over well when we did find her and I had to interrogate her. Everyone who knows her father, hell, who knows she's an officer's kid, would know that I was interrogating her. It wasn't going to be a good time and I was going to get some shit about it even after the truth came out. I was fully prepared for it, though, and it didn't matter what other cops thought. This was about keeping people safe and making sure a skeleton key that could wipe out our country was prevented.

My phone rang and I pulled it out to see that it was Sebastian calling me. "Hey, tell me you have something good," I pleaded into the phone the second I picked up.

"Two things. The first, we were able to find the crew's latest heist. It was another jewelry store that was not on our list. Turns out they are completely legit, but when you go into their basement it is filled with conflict diamonds and stolen pieces. The crew made off with ten million this time."

"Jesus fuck."

This crew's plan was working and as long as it was working, they were not going to be changing it. My gut said they would already be scooping out another kid to grab and I had no idea who it could be.

"Second, we found Jessica, or technically, she found us. She walked into a police station about an hour ago crying and putting on a huge show. Her father is with her now, and they are going to be brought into the Agency to be interviewed."

Son of a bitch.

She knew she couldn't be kidnapped the whole time. She would have to be found at some point.

Why not control when she was discovered by her showing up claiming to have escaped?

She was clearly going to keep up with her show and I was going to have to break her. I just hoped that her father would allow me to do it. I would have to interview her with him out of the room. She would feel comfortable and protected with her father there with her. I needed her to feel the pressure of the reality she was facing. Though, it would help if we had something that I could use as proof to get her to open up.

"I'm on my way," I said, before I ended the call. I then quickly dialed Cooper's number to see if he had anything.

"Hey," he said, and I could already hear the exhaustion in his voice. I might have kept him up too late last night.

Oops.

"Jessica just walked into a police station an hour ago. Apparently, she put on a big show about being kidnapped. She is being taken to the Agency with her father for an interview. I am heading there now. Tell me you have something that I can use against her."

"Okay, so I was able to get all of the other five hacker's names from Drew. I ran the names and was able to get a match on each one. The other four hackers are spread out across the country. I've sent their names off to

Agents so they can be picked up and questioned. They won't be in trouble, all are minors, but they need to be made aware of the situation. Now, all of the conversations in the chat room are gone, they delete automatically after a few hours. However, with the help of Drew, I was able to narrow down each part that was assigned to each hacker for the skeleton key. Now, Jessica doesn't know that I wasn't able to open her hidden files, so you could bluff her."

"She's only fourteen, she should be easy to bluff. What was her part?"

If I could get her alone, then I would be able to bluff her. She was young, she wouldn't know how to control her emotions or be able to keep her lies straight. If I could get the truth out of her, it wouldn't matter what anyone said.

"She is an information hacker. Their specialty is to curate information."

"How is that a hacker?" I asked, confused.

"Information hackers aren't building lists of cigarette brands. They go into a company's system to generate information that could be used against them. Take a bank, for example. The hacker will get every single name of everyone who is hired by the bank, their physical characteristics, age, marital status, social security number, their parents, mother's maiden name, any pets, literally everything about their life. They will then sell that information to someone looking to do a heist, or they steal their identity and steal tens of thousands of dollars from them. Information hackers can be very dangerous. I once arrested one who stole three cents a day out of a million bank accounts. Made thirty grand a day and they did it for a year before anyone caught on."

"Wow, okay. Well, that explains why our hacker liked her so much. She could have made millions of dollars for him. What would she have been collecting for the skeleton key?"

"Like I said, most of everything is done online, but there are main hubs for power that have to be done in person. Unless you want to make a big explosion by sending in a team with guns, you would want someone to take over someone's identity. If she could gather the proper intel, they could put one of their own guys into the hub and turn the power off for a third of the country. Based on the large size of the hidden files, she was putting the intel into a video game that would then be released into the DarkNet for the hacker."

"Got it. All right, I'm going to speak with her and see if we can get the crew or the hacker from her. Keep me posted if you find something else."

"Will do."

I ended the call and started to make my way toward the Agency. I now had something that I would be able to use against Jessica and I was hoping it would work. The last thing I needed was Officer Montanna trying to shut down the interrogation or demand that she had a lawyer.

***

The second I walked into the Agency's interrogation area I could tell that Officer

Montanna was annoyed. He didn't appreciate that he was down here with his daughter as opposed to in an office upstairs. I knew this wasn't going to be easy for him to hear, but there were no other options right now. We needed to get Jessica talking and, hopefully, identify this robbery crew or the hacker.

"Officer Montanna, I appreciate you coming down here with your daughter. I know it's been a trying couple of days for the both of you," I said as I held my hand out to him. I didn't need to introduce myself, he was well aware of who I was.

"Thank you Detective West. I am glad to hear that your son was okay."

"Thank you. He's doing really well. I know you want to get Jessica home, but given the targets this kidnapping and robbery crew are after, we need to catch them before another kid is grabbed. If I could just speak with Jessica for a few minutes, I would truly appreciate it."

"Of course, we're happy to help."

I guided them over to an empty interrogation room and led them both in. I didn't sit down, though, or close the door as I spoke. "This is Damien. He works with the Agency. He is going to speak with you, Officer Montanna."

He looked over my shoulder and saw Damien behind me. Instantly, I could see the objection in his body language. He was not going to go quietly on this one.

"I am staying with my daughter. He can speak with me later."

"I understand your reluctance to leave your daughter, but I'm not actually asking. It's an order," I said with complete authority to my voice.

He could take Jessica and leave, but that would not go well for him. The Agency didn't need a warrant to question or hold her. If he wanted this to go smoothly, he would have no choice but to cooperate.

"Follow me, Officer," Damien said with a deadly edge to his voice.

Officer Montanna looked at us both before he turned to look at Jessica. He then gave a nod and headed out behind Damien. I knew he wasn't going to be going far, just on the other side of the two-way mirror. I wanted to make sure he heard what was going on so if Jessica tried to stonewall me, he would be able to help me get it out of her. I just needed him to hear the evidence first, before jumping to his daughter's defense. I also needed Jessica to speak freely, something she would be more open to doing with her father out of the room.

I closed the door and just leaned against it. I was in charge, not her. She looked scared, but I couldn't tell if it was all an act or not. I suspected a bit of both.

"Why don't you drop the act. We both know you weren't kidnapped," I started, and instantly she was upset and putting on another show.

"What are you talking about? I was kidnapped. I got grabbed by these men right out of my bed and then tied to a chair. I was there for over a day. I was screaming for help, but no one could hear me."

"You were screaming? How did you get the duct tape off of your mouth?"

"They didn't put any on me. They tied my wrists and ankles down to the chair with rope and then they put a gag around my mouth. I was able to spit it out and scream for help. But no one came."

"How did you get out of the chair if you were tied down?" I countered.

"I fought against the ropes and was able to finally get it loose enough on my wrists. It took forever."

"You're lying," I said as I started to move around the room.

"No, I'm not. Why do you keep saying that?" she asked, with tears rolling down her cheeks. No doubt she suspected that she was being watched and wanted to put on a good show for the camera.

"Because I was there when Drew was found. I was the one who cut the ropes off of his wrists. I know how tight they were. And even though he didn't fight against them, his wrists and ankles were red and burned from the rope. If you did, in fact, fight free of the rope, your wrists would not only be red, but also bloody from cutting into your skin. You have no marks on them. You were never gagged and you were never tied up. You were never kidnapped. You faked the whole thing."

"No I didn't. What is wrong with you? I am a victim. I was kidnapped, I could have been killed. Why are you doing this to me?"

"You are putting on a good show, but that's all that it is. Do you really think I would bring you down here without any proof? You're done, Jessica."

"I don't know what you are talking about. I'm a victim and you can't keep me here. I know my rights."

"Your rights went out the door the second your father brought you in here.

This Agency has full immunity from the Governor. I can throw you in jail right now, if I want to. I don't need a warrant or probable cause to arrest you and charge you. And I know you were the one who destroyed your home. That you were the one who destroyed your laptop, or I should say *tried* to destroy it. But you see, the thing with laptops, unless you have obliterated it, someone smart can always rebuild it and recover the data. You might think you're good at hacking, but you are nothing compared to the hacker who works here. He rebuilt your laptop. He found your browser history. He found you playing on the DarkNet. He found your chat room for that hacking workshop you signed up for. He found your hidden files with the video game that you designed to upload onto the DarkNet filled with information that will help to build a skeleton key and start Armageddon. We have it all. You're done. So, drop the helpless victim act, you're not fooling anyone, and Daddy isn't here to save you."

I could see her processing the words and it didn't take long before the tears dried up and she was no longer a scared little teenage girl there in front of me, but rather someone with cold eyes. She was still thinking because she was a teenager that she would be able to get away with it all. That no one would charge her with anything. Unfortunately for her, that would only be true if she cooperated.

"My father wouldn't save me no matter what. He stopped caring about me a long time ago. When Mom was alive, he was working day shifts so he could be home with us at night. He would leave for work after breakfast and be there just after I got home from school. We got to have two meals every day together. I actually got to see him. But two days after Mom dies, he goes back to work and starts working night shifts. I almost never saw him. I was left with a babysitter all night and now that I'm old enough, I don't see anyone at home. Even on his days off he's working. He's doing everything he can to not be around me. He doesn't love me. If he did, he would be there."

"I saw your Dad's timesheets. He's working a lot of overtime, close to sixty hour weeks. But he's not doing it because he doesn't love you. He's doing it because when you work the night shift you get a two dollar premium an hour for working at night because it's more dangerous and the hours suck. That two bucks might not seem like a lot, but that's an extra eighty a week, before the overtime kicks in. Eighty a week might not seem like much to you, but it's three hundred and twenty dollars a month, just shy of four grand a year, and in four years it'll be over fifteen grand that he would have saved up. That's almost a full year of College tuition. *Your* College tuition. Your father loves you. He's working himself to the bone to be able to give you a future."

If she cared about the new information, she didn't show it. I doubted that she cared about the reasoning behind her father's working hours. To her, it wouldn't be a good enough excuse. She would turn it around to make it seem like her father didn't love her. That she was a poor little girl being abandoned by her own father. She was going to work it in her favor. She was going to twist everything that her father did to make it seem like she was neglected.

"I don't need him to pay for my College. I could get student loans, not that I actually want to go. I have a real skill that is very valuable. Companies all over the world are going to want me to work for them. I'll be making millions of dollars a year. I don't need College," she said, a cocky smirk plastered on her lips.

"You are aware that hacking is illegal. Unless you are a Government Agent or work in the military, you are committing a crime. And that's not even including you working with four other hackers to create a skeleton key. Something that can be considered an act of terrorism and have you placed in a maximum federal prison for the rest of your life. The only way to avoid that, is by telling me everything you know about the kidnapping crew and the hacker bchind it all."

"But, Detective, I'm just a little girl," she said, flashing me that cocky smile again.

Before I could even respond to her, the door to the room was opening and Officer Montanna was walking in. I could see the hurt and shock in his eyes. This was why I wanted him to hear what she had to say when she thought he wasn't around. I needed him to hear the truth right out of her mouth. For him to see that she was behind her own kidnapping and that there were serious charges laid in front of her.

"Dad?"

"Jessica, what have you done? I just

heard everything. You faked your own kidnapping. You have been hacking and exploring the DarkNet. Did you really help make this skeleton key thing?"

"I haven't done anything wrong. I was doing an online workshop to learn how to hack. I didn't do anything wrong."

"Except you knew that the skeleton key wasn't actually going to be used in a virtual simulation. You knew the mastermind behind all of this was going to use it in real practice," I argued.

"What— what is it?" Officer Montanna asked.

"It's a complex code that requires multiple parts to be put together in order for it to be created. However, once you have it created, you can hack into anything that is connected to the Internet. You can also copy it onto a USB drive to plug it into any hub and hack into it. It can be used for the Stock Market, all the way to the Nuclear Launch Codes. The person could use the skeleton key to send us all back into the Dark Ages, or use it to drop nukes on any country in the world and start World War Three," I explained.

"Oh my god," Officer Montanna said as he started to pace around the small room.

"Your daughter is the one who provided our mastermind with the intel he needed to ensure he would be able to have access to any location that was not connected to the Internet. She was an active member of the group and has helped to create it. Her part was already handed over. The only reason it was not finished, is because Drew's part wasn't finished. He didn't do it. He felt like something was wrong and he wasn't about to do something that created a world danger," I started as I went and turned the chair around and sat down in it. "But see, that's where it gets interesting. Because Drew is one of a few in a small circle of hackers who can create, from scratch, an algorithm that can adapt and change depending on the system the skeleton key is being used for. It's very mathematical and complicated and the mastermind can't do it. That's why he was kidnapped and left alone. He was going to be moved and then convinced to do his part. As for you, you played kidnapped so the crew could steal ten million in illegal diamonds."

"Drew betrayed our hive. He knew that going into the final project that his part was vital to completion. He betrayed us. He betrayed our family that Danthor has created for us," Jessica said.

Bingo.

We now had a name for our hacker and I knew that Cooper would be able to track him with it now.

"What are you doing? Jessica, that crew kidnapped someone, they have stolen twelve million dollars worth of diamonds. They are facing multiple felony charges that could get them twenty-five plus years in prison. You can be charged as an accomplice to it all. In addition to being an accomplice for helping to create a skeleton key. Detective West is right, you could be charged with crimes against the country. It doesn't matter that you're fourteen, you can be charged as an adult at your age. You wouldn't be the first fourteen year old to be charged as an adult."

Officer Montanna was beyond pissed, not that I could blame him. However, I could also hear the fear and worry in his voice and concern over what future was laid out in front of his daughter. He understood how serious the situation was. How dangerous the situation was for his daughter. He let out a sigh, then he went and sat in the other chair right next to his daughter, before he continued.

"The robbery crew and the mastermind have not been arrested. That means that you can tell Detective West everything you know and you can get a deal. You can avoid going to jail or juvie. We could make a deal for probation and we can put all of this behind us. We can fix this together. You just have to tell us what you know."

"What I know is that Danthor loves me. I'm not going to turn on him. He hasn't done anything wrong. He would never use the skeleton key to hurt anybody. We're going to use it to catch criminals that the justice system has failed to put away. He's not a bad guy," Jessica said, still not willing to give any of them up.

"Jessica, he doesn't love you. He's just a predator using you. It's not a coincidence that you were the only female who got to move on. He is a predator and he is using you for your skills. Everything he told you was a lie, even down to whatever age he said he was. He doesn't love you. You're just someone he can manipulate and leave to take the fall for this whole mess," I said.

I had a feeling, though, that no matter what either of us said, Jessica wasn't going to give them up. She was completely at Danthor's mercy. He had her wrapped around his finger and she was going to keep believing in his cause. She was going to keep believing that the court wouldn't put her in prison for any of these crimes. The thing was, though, they would. This wasn't what I wanted, but this was the path she wanted to walk. Hopefully, she would change her mind soon. Maybe after she spent the night in jail, she would think twice about her decision to stay quiet.

"I'm sorry," I said to Officer Montanna and I could see he understood what would happen. "Jessica Montanna, you are under arrest for two counts of grand larceny, one count of kidnapping, and an accessory to crimes against the country. You have the right to remain silent. You have the right to an attorney. If you cannot afford one, one will be provided to you. Do you understand your rights?"

"Sure," she said as she rolled her eyes.

"Where... where will she go?" Officer Montanna asked with a shaky voice as I went and put the cuffs on Jessica.

"She will be taken to the county juvenile hall, where she will be held until her court date. Due to the charges, though, she won't be eligible for bail. Unless she decides to plead out, it could take a year before her trial date."

"Chill out, Dad, I won't be there for a year. Danthor won't let me be in jail for more than a day or two. He'll hack the system and make sure someone comes to get me," Jessica said with that snarky attitude still dripping from her voice.

"No, he won't. But maybe a couple of days rooming with criminals will teach you that," I said as I started to walk her to the door. It opened and I passed her off to Damien who would take her the rest of the way.

"I'm so sorry," Officer Montanna instantly said when we were alone.

"You have nothing to apologize for. Her actions are not your responsibility. I'm sorry that things turned out this way. Hopefully, the night in jail will make her realize the seriousness of her situation and she will sing."

"I should have seen this coming. I shouldn't have changed my shift. I would have been there more."

"Don't do that. You can't second-guess yourself. This isn't your fault. She was manipulated by a predator who has done this before. We will find him and make sure he pays for all of this. Get her a good lawyer and maybe a therapist in the jail. Maybe, they will be able to get her to see what is really going on."

Whether I liked what Jessica had done didn't matter. She was still a fourteen year old girl who had been taken advantage of by an adult male. She had no idea just how serious this situation was because she wasn't old enough to understand the true implications of it. Hopefully, with time and some professional help, she would, and then she would be more open to talking. For now, we had to focus all of our efforts on finding the kidnapping crew and Danthor before they all disappeared.

CHAPTER FOURTEEN

Cooper

IT WAS NEARING eight o'clock when Jonah walked through the door. He looked exhausted and I had a feeling that meant his interrogation with Jessica had not been an easy one.

He had texted me Danthor's name, but that was all he had said. He told me he would tell me once he got back. I had been spending the day with Drew, trying to find the other hackers from the workshop, and trying to find the mastermind based off of the YouTube video.

What concerned me, was the number of views the video had. It had over two million views, and even if people didn't watch it all the way through, it was still a huge pool of potential hackers that this man had been cultivating from his workshop. Even if only twenty percent of the people who viewed the video took the workshop, it was a large number of hackers that he could have at his beck and call.

Thankfully, what was needed to finish the skeleton key was not something your garden variety hacker could pull off. We were most likely still in the clear with him not having it completed.

"You okay, Dad?" Drew asked, with a great deal of concern lacing his voice.

"Yeah, I'm okay. It was just a long conversation and it didn't go the way I was expecting or hoped it would."

"She didn't know anything?" I asked.

"Oh, she knows something, but she's not talking. She believes that Danthor loves her and that they were going to use the skeleton key to get justice for those that the justice system has failed. He has her completely snowed. Even after Officer Montanna came into the room, she wouldn't give anything up. She is on her way to juvie and hopefully, after spending the night there, she will realize that Danthor isn't coming for her."

"She really won't give anything up?" Drew asked, surprised.

"Not even after we told her the charges. Because of what the skeleton key can do, she could be charged for acts of terrorism. She's facing life, but she believes she will be saved by the love of her life. She's a young and dumb fourteen year old girl who got played by a predator. It happens, unfortunately, and by the time she realizes what happened to her, it most likely will be too late for her to make a deal. I just feel bad for Officer Montanna. He went through the trauma and horror of having his only child kidnapped, only to discover it was all fake and now, she will be spending her life in prison."

"It's not something any parent should have to go through. Maybe her lawyer will be able to talk some sense into her," I said.

It wasn't that surprising, though, that

she didn't give anyone up. Like Jonah said, she was young and dumb, and had been manipulated by an older man. Danthor knew exactly what he was doing when he recruited her. It was going to take a long time before she would finally give it up, and I had no idea if it was ever going to happen in time for her to save herself.

"Hopefully. What do you got?"

"We found the other four hackers and they were all picked up by Homeland Security Agents and brought back to the field offices for questioning. I heard back from all four agents, all four hackers did their part of the skeleton key and submitted it onto the DarkNet in a video game format already. Now, all four said they had no idea it was going to be turned into a real functioning key. They all believed that a security company or a recruitment office for Government Agencies was running the workshop. The Agents weren't sure if they believed them, so they were all hooked up to a polygraph test and they all passed. They were all under eighteen, most were fifteen or sixteen, and they will be placed on a watch list. They were all offered the opportunity to use their skills for good when they turn eighteen, should they be interested. Who knows if they will be, though," I stated.

It was good that Homeland was offering them a position in their academy, but I also knew that not every hacker wanted to be buff and attend boot camp to get a job as a hacker. It would depend on their personality and if they truly wanted to do some good in the world. If not, they could keep being a hacker for a company, a black hat hacker, or they could stop all together and go work for a tech firm. Really, their futures were completely up in the air, but we might have saved four young hackers from going down a bad path.

"At least that's something. Did they know anything we could use?"

"No, they just knew the name Danthor. They had no idea that there was a kidnapping/robbery crew out there. They did say that Danthor paid more attention to Jessica in the chat room. He was always praising her and sending her bitcoins as a reward for her learning efforts."

"Which supports our theory that he had been courting her to manipulate her into being his puppet. Where are we on finding him?"

"*Nowhere*. We are nowhere. It's great that we have his hacker name, but just like in real life, having just a name and no photo to put it with makes it very difficult to track the guy down. He could be anywhere, and with just a hacker name, I can't even run it in a system to see what pops. I have to work the DarkNet to try and track down his movements and see if anyone has been able to see him, and try to get his real name to then use to track down in the real world. It's not something that is going to be a quick resolution. It could take years to find him."

That was the issue. When we had a suspect, we had their name that we could then run. Then, we find their photo online, either from social media or a driver's license. With just a hacker name,

I couldn't run it through our databases. It was going to take a long time and a lot of work to track down someone who could give me his real name and then, I could try and get a photo of him to run in the system. It wasn't something that was magically going to get done within hours or even weeks.

"That's not good. He could have a skeleton key finished by then," Jonah said, clearly worried.

"I informed Mason about all of this and he told Ryzen. Ryzen used to work for the CIA and he got into contact with some of his connections there. They then reached out to me. The other Agents sent in the video games that were uploaded from the four other hackers, plus one of the hackers knew what video game Jessica had uploaded to the DarkNet. I created an algorithm-coded virus that would completely destroy the video games and any information within. The CIA hacker was able to adapt their own code to my virus so it would destroy any information gathered from the video games that was uploaded onto any computer. So even though we don't know who Danthor is, all of his work for the skeleton key is completely destroyed."

It was very complex and I could tell that Jonah had no idea what I was talking about, but all that mattered was that the skeleton key was destroyed and if Danthor wanted to create one, he would have to start all over again and with new hackers. At least it was buying us time.

We would also, hopefully, be able to get into the chat room for the last workshop and shut it down with the help of the other four hackers. Drew no longer had access to it because he left, but the other four hadn't left yet. From what I had been told, they were all willing to cooperate with Homeland to get it all shut down.

"I understood that last part of that. That's good, though. That means he will have to start from square one and that buys us the time we need to, hopefully, track him down. He's not going to give up, not when he was so close to having it made."

A loud beeping interrupted our conversation and I instantly knew what it was. My fingers flew over my keyboard as Drew spoke.

"What is that?"

"I'm being hacked," I answered.

I knew it had to be Danthor trying to

get into my system. Only, my system wasn't like the ones that he was used to. Mine was far more complex and sophisticated than a typical security system. He wasn't going to be able to hack in, but I might be able to pinpoint his location while he was busy trying to get into my system.

"If he's trying to hack in, that means the kidnappers are coming here. They might be trying to get Drew to make the skeleton key," Jonah said. He was up and already looking out my front window.

"They won't be able to get in if they are. The doors can't be hacked and there's no lock to pick. Even if they tried to shoot their way in, the windows are all bulletproof," I said.

"Why do you have bulletproof windows?" Drew asked, completely confused and scared.

"Because I've put a lot of dangerous criminals away and they would love to have me killed."

"We got company. There's four masked guys right outside and they have automatic weapons. It seems like Danthor told them we were on to them and now they want us dead," Jonah said as he pulled out his phone.

"Okay, but if they can't get in, then don't we just wait for the cops to show up?" Drew said.

"That's what we're doing," Jonah said as he moved back before speaking into the phone. "This is Detective West, I'm at 1223 Southshore Lane, the kidnapping crew is at my location. I'm secured in the house with my son. Four men are armed with automatic weapons. Have everyone available to roll out to my location."

"Dammit," I said.

"What?" Jonah asked as he put his phone away.

"He disappeared. He must have figured out that he couldn't hack in and he left before I could trace him."

I wasn't expecting for him to give up that easily. Once he saw my system, he had to know that they wouldn't be able to just waltz right in. I would have figured he would have tried harder, but he just gave up.

"Um, what is that?" Drew asked and we both looked to see what he was looking at out the window.

The one man had opened the trunk and pulled out an RPG. "Shit, yup that's a flaw," I said with urgency.

We both jumped into action and

started to move away from the window. We were only going to have a few seconds before that thing was flying into my house. We both pulled out guns and flipped the dining room table over before the three of us got behind it. Then, there was an explosion and the sound of glass shattering throughout the front of my house. My ears were instantly ringing and I knew it wouldn't be long before the bullets would be flying. Thankfully, there were only four of them, but they had automatic weapons, making it feel more like twenty guys. I could hear the dull sound of the bullets flying toward us and Jonah covered Drew's body with his own. The wooden table was not going to do anything to protect us. We had to move.

"Get behind the island," I yelled at them.

Jonah was instantly pushing Drew to move and I poked my head up enough to be able to provide cover fire. We also only had one clip each, so we had to make each shot count. The second they were behind the island, I was moving. I managed to take out one of the kidnappers in the process and I was relieved that we were down to three. All we had to do was hold them off long enough for backup to arrive.

"Dad!" Drew cried, and I turned my head to see a large blood pool forming underneath Jonah.

He had been hit.

Most likely when he was protecting Drew behind the table.

Shit.

I moved my hand over and checked for a pulse. It was there, but it was weak. I grabbed one of the towels that were hanging on the bottom cupboards as I spoke. "Drew, listen to me. I need you to push this against the bullet wound. Push as hard as you can to try and slow the bleeding down. Backup will be here soon."

Drew took the towel with trembling hands and pushed it against the lower part of Jonah's back. I was worried that the bullet could have hit his spine. I knew he had moved over to behind the island, but that could have pushed the bullet around more into his spine. There was no telling what damage could be done and we wouldn't know until a doctor was able to run scans.

None of that could happen while we were trapped here.

I didn't have my phone, but Jonah had placed his in his pocket. I quickly pulled it out and keyed the radio option for his phone.

"This is Agent Jones, I need immediate assistance 1223 Southshore Lane. I have an officer down. I repeat, an officer has been shot. We are taking on heavy fire. I need a bus on a rush to my location and every available unit in the area. Start an officer down protocol, and notify Med."

I dropped the phone and started to fire back as the calls came in. Every available unit was responding that they were on their way. I knew within moments the street was going to be flooded with cops, whether they were needed or not. Every cop within a decent distance of our location would be coming here to see if there was anything they could do to help. When it was one of their own down and needing help, they all came.

I could already hear the sirens and I knew we would be getting out of here. I just had to hold them off a bit longer.

"Talk to me, Drew, how is he?" I said as I returned fire again. I needed to keep them back so they wouldn't be able to approach. If they got too close, they could easily kill me and take Drew.

"I don't know," Drew said, his voice warbly and panicked, and I didn't need to look at him to know that he was crying.

This was not what I wanted him to see or go through, but there was nothing I could do about it right now. Right now, we just had to get through this, and then, Jonah would be able to be in the hospital where the doctors could, hopefully, save his life.

"I know this is hard, but help is coming. I can hear the sirens, can you?"

"Yeah," he said with a shaky voice and a sniffle.

I could hear more gunshots, but this time they weren't from an automatic weapon. Help had arrived and I knew it wouldn't take anytime at all before the last few guys were down.

A long series of single gunshots echoed all throughout my house and I knew there were at least ten cops all firing at once. With the last gunshot, the whole house went quiet and I knew we were safe.

"Back here!" I called out as I turned my attention to Jonah.

I took over for Drew as the officers made their way around to my island. I could tell they were shocked by the sight in front of them, but they snapped out of it quickly. The one officer went over to Drew and moved him away, getting him out of the house where he wouldn't have to see the carnage. Another two officers joined me in keeping Jonah stabilized as we waited for the ambulance to arrive.

I could feel my own body shaking. I couldn't believe this had happened. I never thought I would have to go through something like this. It had been a long time since I had been involved in a shootout and never one quite like this. I was terrified about what would happen with Jonah. I knew the gunshot wound was bad and I was very afraid that he wouldn't be able to pull through on this one.

He had just come into my life.

I couldn't lose him.

Not now.

Once the paramedics arrived, I was pushed out of the way and I had no choice but to watch as they fought to save Jonah's life.

***

My back was killing me, the same as my ass. I had been sitting in an uncomfortable plastic hospital chair for twelve hours now. The whole waiting room was filled with cops and the guys from the Agency. We were all waiting on news about Jonah.

He had been rushed into surgery the second the paramedics got him off of the ambulance and so far, we hadn't heard anything yet. I knew no news was good news, but at this point I would have really appreciated something. Even if that was just a nurse coming out to say he was still alive and they were still working on him. At least that would have been something.

As for the case, all four kidnappers were dead. All dead at my house that was now not only a crime scene, but looked like it had been in a war zone. I was going to be moving. There was no way I was going to ever be able to live in that house again. Even if I repaired it, I would always be able to see Jonah's blood all over my kitchen floor. It was better to sell it and let someone else deal with it all. I would make sure it was professionally cleaned and I would have a new wall put up, but I wouldn't be living in it.

Damien, Sebastian, and Max were able to identify the kidnappers and found the stolen diamonds at the stash house they had all been staying in. We had been hoping to get something out of the kidnappers that would lead us to Danthor, but that intel died with them. I suspected Danthor knew that would be the case. And even if they were able to succeed in killing Jonah and I to get to Drew, he would have still won.

As for Drew, he was a mess, but I couldn't blame the kid. He was only twelve and he just went through a shootout that resulted in his father being seriously shot. He would be thinking worst case scenario and terrified for what the future could hold. I hadn't told him it would be okay, because I didn't know and I didn't want to lie to him. I needed to know what Jonah's situation was first before I tried to comfort the poor boy.

The second a doctor walked out to us, we were all on our feet. He came over to me as Drew was standing next to us and without a next of kin, he would have to tell Drew.

"I am Dr. Charles. I was the surgeon for your father. I want to let you know that he is alive and I do expect for him to make a full recovery."

The second the words were out of his mouth there was a palpable great relief that flooded through the entire room. Officers started to hug each other and clap at the good news. I was beyond relieved, but I also knew that depending on where the bullet hit, that recovery could be a very long and painful one.

"Where did the bullet hit?" I asked.

"It hit the bottom of his spine and ended up moving just slightly. From what I was told, he moved for better cover and that is probably when the extra damage was done. I was able to remove the bullet and repair the damage to his spine and the nerves. He will be able to return to active duty in time. However, it's going to be closer to six months before that happens. Due to the damage and the repair, he will need extensive physical therapy to relearn how to walk again."

"He's paralyzed?" Drew asked, horrified.

"He's not paralyzed. He can feel his legs and he can move them. However, his nerves and muscles need to relearn the movement of walking. He's going to be in the hospital for six weeks before he will be able to be released. He will be in a wheelchair until he progresses in his physical therapy and relearns how to walk. I know it sounds scary, but your father is otherwise healthy and he is still young. He will blow through the physical therapy faster than you think. Within six months, he'll be back to running and be active," Dr. Charles said, flashing us all a warm, comforting smile.

I wrapped my arm around Drew's shoulders as I spoke. "All that matters is that he is alive and will make a full recovery. We'll get him through the rest."

"Can I see him?" Drew asked Dr. Charles.

"Of course. I'll take you to him. He's not awake yet, but he will be within a few hours."

We followed the Doctor down the hallways until we reached the recovery room for Jonah.

He looked pale as a ghost, but I knew that was from the blood loss. He had a blood bag as well as an IV to help get some blood back into him. It was going to be a long road ahead of him, but I was determined to make sure he got there.

"What's gonna happen to me?" Drew asked as we went and plopped down into a chair at his father's bedside.

"You're gonna be okay. While your dad is healing, you are gonna be living with me. For now, we'll be in a hotel until I find a new house. Then, when your dad can leave, he'll live with us and we can get him through this. In a few days, when you feel ready, you can go back to school and start getting back to a normal life."

I knew it wasn't going to be easy for him to do that. He had been through a lot in the past couple of days, but eventually, he would get there. We all would get there. I was not about to let either of the West men go through this alone. We were family now and we would get through this as a family.

EPILOGUE

Six Months Later…

Jonah

THE HOUSE WAS filled with people from the Agency.

Today, we were celebrating my return to active duty. The past six months had been life changing, to say the least. Waking up in the hospital to discover that I had not only been shot, *again*, but had to relearn how to walk, well, it was a lot.

I'd had a great deal of some not so proud moments when I snapped at Coop or one of the nurses during my stay at the hospital and even afterward. I wasn't used to not being able to do things on my own. I wasn't used to not being able to move around how I wanted, having to use a wheelchair and then a walker.

Fuck yeah, it was hard.

It was the hardest thing I had ever had to do and it was not something I wanted to ever have to do again.

Over the past six months, though, I had discovered just how much I had fallen in love with Cooper. I didn't even know it, but I was. Seeing him every day at the hospital, seeing him interacting with Drew, it only warmed my heart.

Knowing that Drew was living with

Cooper and going back to school, that he was starting to heal from it all, it only confirmed that Cooper was the perfect man. He loved my son, he cared for him, and he would be an amazing dad to him.

I didn't want to die, I didn't want to leave Drew, but if it did happen, then I could do so knowing he would be loved and well cared for. That Cooper would make sure he had a bright future and would recover from the loss one day. And that was all I wanted for him.

Cooper and I had decided to try our hand at dating after I got out of the hospital. I wasn't sure if it would be a good idea. I mean, I wasn't exactly a catch with being stuck in a wheelchair, but he wouldn't hear any of it.

We had taken things slow. With me not being able to have sex, we were able to learn a great deal about each other. We grew something real that would only make the sex better. And when we finally could have sex last month, it was earth shattering. I thought the previous times were good, but they were nothing compared to the build up and wait over the past five months.

The man was perfect.

Absolutely perfect.

Even when I was able to be living on my own again, neither I nor Drew wanted to leave. This had become our home, a home for all three of us. Thankfully, Cooper was in agreement with us. Drew had even decided to change schools to one within the area. He was ready for a change and he didn't want to be the kid who got kidnapped at his old school. I could understand that. He wanted a fresh start and I was more than happy to give it to him.

Drew was set to attend hackers camp in a couple of weeks for the summer. He was already packed and excited for it. He was like a little kid on Christmas Eve all over again and it was such a relief to see. He had found something that he was not only good at, but passionate about.

There had been many nights that Drew and Cooper would practice hacking into things and Cooper would let him help on the cases he was working on. I had discovered that Cooper would actually pose as an underage kid in different chat rooms to help catch predators. He would then pass off the information to the local police for them to catch the guy when he went to meet up with who he thought was an underage minor. It was just further proof of what a good man he was.

He was a tremendous role model for Drew and I was so happy that he could have Cooper in his life. That he could have an adult in his life who understood what he was talking about and could show him different tricks and skills with a computer. Drew was learning a lot and his attitude was so different. He was back to being a happy and fun kid, and it was all thanks to Cooper.

"Have you thought more about my offer?" Mason asked as he strolled over to me.

Mason had offered me a position within the Agency a couple of months ago. I hadn't given him an answer yet, because I wasn't sure how I felt about it. I still needed time to get my head wrapped around everything that had happened and what I was feeling. Now, though, I did have an answer for him.

"I have and I am going to accept it," I said, flashing him a warm smile.

I would miss being a detective, but I would still be doing what I loved for the Agency. The only difference was, I would have more freedom to do it. I would also be going after criminals who were out to hurt children and that was something I was passionate about. It was time for a change and I liked knowing I would be getting to spend more time with Cooper. We made a good team and I was looking forward to my future within the Agency.

"Perfect. You start tomorrow. Be prepared to be busy. We have cases coming at us from all directions," Mason warned before he headed off.

I knew they were getting busy. Mason

had been trying to find more people to work for him. From what I had heard, Sebastian, Damien, and Max were looking to move down here to help out as well. It should be interesting and I did like working with the guys. I was looking forward to seeing what life had in store for me.

There was one thing that I needed to do today, though, and with some luck it would be another reason to celebrate. I had already spoken to Drew about it and he was over the moon excited. We were both hoping this would turn out well and go the way we wanted it to.

"Excuse me, can I have everyone's attention, please?" I called out into the backyard.

Everyone with the Agency was here and they all turned to look my way. I let out a small sigh, trying to get my nerves to calm down. I had only ever done this once, but I didn't mean it that time. This time, I was going to mean it and I had no idea what I would do if he said no.

"Thank you so much for coming out today and celebrating my return to work. And it looks like I am going to be seeing a lot of you, because I have accepted Mason's offer to work for the Agency." I paused as everyone clapped or cheered. Once they quieted down I spoke again.

"There are a lot of reasons to celebrate today, but I am hoping to add one more." I turned to Cooper and took his hand in mine, my eyes finding his.

"Cooper Jones, I was not expecting you. After my last failed marriage, I never thought I would want to date someone ever again. But then you came into my life when I least expected it. You came into my son's life when he needed you the most. You saved him and you saved me in ways I cannot begin to explain. I can't imagine my life without you being in it. I want to wake up every morning with you in my arms. I want to fall asleep every night holding you against me. I want you to be my last kiss, my last love." I got down onto my knee and pulled out a ring box, opening it as I continued.

"Cooper Jones, will you do me the honor of being my husband?"

I could see the tears building in his eyes. He wasn't expecting this. I couldn't blame him, I never thought I would get married again, either, but I couldn't imagine not having him in my life. I wanted to call him my husband. I wanted everyone to know that he was mine and I was his. I wanted to get married for love this time. I wanted it to last and there was no one I wanted to do that with more than him.

"Yes," he said with a huge smile, happy tears slipping down his cheeks.

Everyone started to clap and cheer as I slipped the ring onto his finger.

I stood and pulled him in for a heated kiss. I didn't care who was watching, he had said *yes* and I was too damn excited to keep it as a simple kiss.

Tonight, though, we would be celebrating this alone and we would be putting our soundproof bedroom to great use. For now, though, we were going to celebrate our new engagement with our family. The future was ours and I couldn't wait.

Thank you for reading!

If you enjoyed Cooper, do me a solid
and go leave a review?
Even a few words can make my day
and give me the motivation to keep on
plugging away at the stories you love.

Thank you!

Next up is Noah!

That's right, we are going to get to know Ryzen's brother a little bit more.

This story is definitely going to be the one that turns up the heat to the super steamy level, so be forewarned.

Turn the page now for a preview, if you dare, but be sure to click and preorder your copy at your favorite online retailer and be one of the first to read Noah's story! Can we just say YUMMY? lol

PREVIEW

Noah

I WALKED INTO the club tonight on a mission. Tonight, I needed sex, but not just any old vanilla sex. I needed to be dominated, manhandled. I needed to find myself a Master.

I didn't care for taking orders outside of the bedroom, but when I was in it, I did enjoy it. Working as a Federal Prosecutor,

I saw some of the worst that humanity had to offer this world. I saw a lot of cases that were forever burned into my brain and I would never be able to stop the nightmares from them.

I always had to be in charge. Always forced to make literal life or death calls. I had to make sure the person I was prosecuting was, in fact, guilty, and then, I had to get the jury to see it. It took everything out of me and left me feeling more exhausted than I could possibly put into words.

So, when it all became too much, when I felt like I couldn't breathe, I would go to a club like the one I'd just walked into and seek out sex with a Dominant. Someone who would dominate and control me. Someone who would make the decisions, so all I had to do was what I was told. There was no thinking involved. There were no lives on the line, no victims in desperate need of justice. It was just him and I and nothing but pleasure. It made my brain turn off and made me feel something other than stressed and sick. After the last few months that I'd had, I needed it now more than ever.

For the past three months, I had been working on a huge case to prosecute a brothel owner who filled his smarmy business with underage girls as prostitutes. It should have been a slam-dunk, but the defendant was claiming he was innocent. That he had no idea those girls weren't eighteen, even though they were clearly fourteen to fifteen. He refused a plea deal, and wanted to take it to trial. And I knew why, too, because at trial the only way we could prove that he had knowledge of their ages would be to have each girl testify.

Out of the dozen girls that he had working for him, young teens that he had raped, abused, and trafficked out to the highest paying customer, only five agreed to testify.

I had to listen to them talk about how he had raped and abused them. How the customers had forced and used them in all sorts of disgusting, sexually deviant ways.

I had them on the stand and testifying, telling their stories, only for his defense attorney to try and make it seem like they were using him. That the girls had lied. The defense kept trying to make it seem like the defendant was the victim in all of this.

He brought up all of their past history,

how they ran away, how they were addicted to drugs. The only reason they were addicted in the first place was because he had forced the heroin into them. He was a monster who had done this before. He had done this in different cities with different girls. He had never been caught. He always shut his brothels down when the heat was starting to get too hot.

We had finally caught him in New York.

We were finally going to be able to put his ass in jail.

We were finally going to be able to stop him.

The jury deliberated for three hours before they came back with a not guilty verdict. They actually believed that he was a victim in this and not the girls.

Not guilty.

After three months of having to listen to their stories, their horrors, only for them to be treated like lying drug addicts who tried to take advantage of a businessman.

Unfuckingbelieveable.

He had a legal license for a brothel, so we couldn't even get him for that. He was off to another State for a whole new set of victims and there was nothing I could do about it.

I was done.

I had put in time for three weeks off, packed a bag, and I was out of there. I didn't even wait for a plane. I just got into my car and drove. It took two days for me to get to Baton Rouge and I was planning on staying at a hotel. I knew I could stay with my brother, Ryzen, but he was busy living with his new boyfriend, Knox. I did not want to hear them having sex.

Plus, this was going to be my vacation. My time to unwind and have as much sex as I wanted. I wanted to be able to do whatever I wanted; if that meant drinking at nine in the morning, if that was what I chose to do, then that's what I was going to do.

I made my way over to the bar and ordered a whiskey from a cute bartender who eyed me up and down with a nod. This was a gay club, but it was one that catered to those that were into the kink lifestyle, doms and subs, mostly. It was a place where you could go and meet a new partner for a single night or even for a new relationship.

I wasn't looking for a relationship, because I would only be here for three weeks. I just wanted some fun. I wanted to feel good and I wanted to not have to think and plan and strategize. I just wanted to escape feeling all of this pain.

I grabbed my drink and turned around to look at the club patrons. I needed to find someone who was clearly a Dom, but was also attractive. I didn't just sleep with anyone. I had a standard and I liked what I liked. I never settled for anything less. If I was going to trust my body with someone, then they were going to have to meet my standards. With that said, I was really hoping someone here tonight would match my standards.

A lot of people were already paired off, so I ignored them and kept scanning the crowd. My gaze landed on a man roughly my age. He was muscular and rugged looking. I liked my Doms to be rough around the edges. I didn't need them pretty, I was man pretty enough for the both of us.

I knew I wasn't a typical submissive. I was a bit bigger than most and I had muscles. I didn't spend all day at the gym, but I did enjoy working out. I kept my gaze on him and his eyes locked onto mine, one brow arching above a chocolate brown eye. He appeared to be interested in me, so I decided to make the first move.

I finished my drink before I strolled out onto the dance floor. I kept my gaze on him as I started to sway my hips, making it clear I was up for some fun. He didn't look away. He kept his eyes on me and I could tell he was enjoying what he saw.

I slowly turned around and started to move more to the music. As I danced, I could already feel my stress starting to melt away. I relaxed more when I was able to be around people who understood me. Men who didn't care what I liked in the bedroom because they enjoyed it as well. It was a few minutes later when I felt strong hands being placed on my hips and his hardness pressed against my ass. I didn't even have to turn around to know it was the man I had been watching. The man I wanted.

I pressed my ass back against him, reveling in the feeling of his already hard dick against my ass. It was big, very big, and that made me extremely excited. He ran his hand down my chest, over stomach, and he didn't stop until his hand skimmed my dick. I couldn't help but moan at the simple touch. It had been close to six months since I'd had sex and I was in desperate need.

"You're already hard, my sweet boy. Tell Daddy what you want," his husky voice growled into my ear.

Daddy, huh?

Hmmm.

That was a new one for me, but it wasn't a turn off. I was used to the typical Master or Sir, I had never had a Daddy. I knew that it was one of the names some Doms liked to be called, though. It wasn't a fetish that involved treating your partner as a child, despite what many people thought. It was more about taking care of their partner, making sure the submissive knew they were safe with the Dominant and felt good. I didn't care what he liked to be called just as long as he made the noise in my head quiet down.

"You feel so big, Daddy. I'd love to feel your dick against my tongue, deep in my ass," I answered as I ground back against him some more, his body heat surrounding me.

"Follow," he ordered, and the command sent shivers up my spine.

"Yes, Daddy."

He took my hand and guided me through the crowd toward the backrooms. This club had ten backrooms that could be used for hookups. It was why I chose this club over the other ones. I was not about to bring anyone back to my hotel room.

The second we walked into the room, Daddy slammed me against the door. He wrapped his hand around my neck and captured my mouth with his own.

I moaned at the roughness and easily kissed him back. I allowed him to have all of the control. I loved it when the man I was with took complete control in the bedroom and Daddy didn't seem to have a single issue with taking what he wanted.

His tongue slipped into my mouth as he deepened the kiss. I couldn't believe how amazing it felt to be kissed after the past six months. He knew exactly how to take control of it and make me feel weak in my knees.

After a moment, when we both needed air, he pulled back, but kept his hand on my neck, his hips pressed to mine as he panted.

"Tell me what you want me to do, Daddy." I said, flashing him a playful smile.

"I want you on your knees with my dick in your mouth, my sweet boy," he ordered.

"Yes, Daddy," I whimpered, before I got

down onto my knees. I was all too happy to take this man in my mouth. I could feel how hard he was against his jeans and I couldn't wait to see his dick uncovered. I knew he was going to be big and I was really hoping he knew how to use it.

I made quick work of popping the button and unzipping his jeans. The second I pulled his hard dick out, I was moaning, my mouth watering at the sight. He was as big as I thought he'd be. He certainly didn't disappoint. Now, I was just hoping that he would be talented with it.

"I love a huge dick, Daddy," I moaned. I ran my tongue along his shaft from his base up to his tip, getting my first taste of him. I took his tip in my mouth and sucked, humming my appreciation as the taste of his precum hit my tongue.

I needed more. I needed to know what Daddy's cum tasted like, what it felt like as it pumped down my throat. I started to work my way down his large shaft.

I was a slutty submissive, and I was proud of it. I had made peace with my desires a long time ago. I also knew that my sexual interests were most likely connected to the lack of a father figure in my life. I didn't care, though, because it felt good and that was all that mattered to me.

I felt Daddy thread his hand into my hair, getting a good grip. I moaned at the slight pull as I worked my way down to Daddy's base.

"You like that?" Daddy asked in a husky voice as he pulled my hair a bit harder this time.

I whimpered as I looked up at Daddy

through heavy-lidded eyes as I pressed my lips around his base, his hardness stretching my throat. I could see the heat in his eyes and I was willing to bet that not many guys would be able to take him all the way into their mouth. But for me, I loved the feeling of a dick in my throat.

"Holy fuck," he moaned as he started to lightly thrust his hips.

I returned the moan as I felt him start to fuck my mouth. I could feel my dick pulse with need as he thrust his hips and his balls slapped my chin. This was exactly what I'd wanted. I'd needed someone to use me for their own pleasure. Someone who could make everything disappear all around me.

Daddy started to move his hips even faster and I felt his dick getting harder, his cockhead swelling. He was getting close to coming and I wanted it desperately. I wanted to drink every last drop he had for me.

Daddy was moaning deeply now, as his pace picked up even more. I knew my throat was going to be sore tomorrow from the abuse, but I didn't care. I would buy lozenges by the dozen just to make this go longer.

After a few more thrusts, Daddy snapped his hips forward and let out a deep growl as he shot line after line of scorching hot cum down my throat. I whimpered like a bitch in heat as I greedily swallowed everything he had for me.

Fuck, he tasted so sweet.

I couldn't remember the last time I had tasted anyone that sweet before. I moved back, pulling him from my throat, and sucked at his tip, getting the last few drops out of him before he pulled out. I instantly mourned the loss of the feeling of his dick against my tongue.

"You taste so good," I moaned out as I licked my lips.

"You're a bit of a cock slut, huh?" Daddy groaned.

"More than a bit," I replied, flashing him a grin before I wrapped my lips around him once more and sucked on his tip again, getting a couple of stray drops of his precious essence. "I could suck your dick all day," I said as I looked up at him.

He pulled me up by my hair with a growl and smashed his lips against mine. He shoved his tongue into my mouth and I moaned as he licked and sucked at my tongue, getting a taste of himself. I could feel the passion and desire within him. He needed more and I was all too happy to oblige. After a moment, he pulled back and spoke.

"Get naked, up on the bed on your hands and knees. I want your ass in the air."

"Yes, Daddy," I moaned.

I quickly began to remove my clothing as Daddy did with his own. I scrambled over to the bed and got into his ordered position while he went around and grabbed the lube from the bedside drawer.

I leaned onto my elbows and spread my legs nice and wide for him, making sure he had the perfect view of my ass. I heard him groan and I knew exactly what he had seen.

He ran his hand down my ass and

pushed on the end of the plug that I had inserted before I left the hotel.

"And what do we have here, my sweet boy?"

"I stretched myself before coming here, Daddy. That way I wouldn't have to be stretched. Plus, I like the feel of it." I moaned, jutting my hips backward as he pushed it in even further.

I found something comforting about having a plug in. I knew it was weird. No, not at the top of the weird scale, but it wasn't normal, either. I had always enjoyed the feeling of having a dick inside of me. I didn't know why and I couldn't explain it, but the fullness, the stretch, always brought me comfort. I felt connected to someone and I had missed that growing up. It was safe to say I had a healthy sex toy collection, some of which

I'd brought with me.

"I like that you enjoy having something inside of you, my sweet boy. So many others deny themselves what they find joy in. It's good for you to embrace it," Daddy said as he ran his hand over my ass.

I felt a light slap to my ass and it caused me to let out a light moan. I did enjoy being spanked, by either a hand or a belt. I enjoyed a bit of pain with my pleasure. Anything to make me feel something other than empty and sad.

"You like it rough, my sweet boy?" he asked as he slapped my ass even harder this time.

"Fuck yes. You can be as rough as you want, Daddy," I said and moaned as I thrust my ass up hoping to encourage him to continue. I wanted more. I *needed* more. I wasn't a masochist by any stretch of the imagination, but I did enjoy the rough and painful sex if there was pleasure with it.

"Good to know," he breathed and chuckled. He slapped me as hard as he could, the sound echoing out in the room and red-hot fire blooming over my skin.

I gave a deep moan and again pushed my ass in the air. "Again, please, Daddy."

He did it again, but this time he also made sure to hit the end of the plug to drive it even further inside of me. The end rubbed my sweet spot and I squealed.

I couldn't help but push my ass out even more. I needed more and Daddy did not disappoint. He continued to slap my ass as hard as he could. White-hot fire burned over my cheeks and thighs and I was already looking forward to seeing the red marks and light bruising there tomorrow. My ass throbbed and I loved every moment of it.

"I'm negative. I've got the proof in my pocket. I got tested last week and I haven't been with anyone since. Tell Daddy it's okay for him to fuck you without a condom." I could hear him panting behind me as he said the words and I knew he was as on edge as I was at that moment.

Usually, my immediate answer to that question would be a solid no. I'd learned not to blindly trust what people said in the heat of the moment, but somehow I knew he wasn't giving me some line.

Call it gut instinct.

He most likely did have those test results in his jeans and I was confident he was negative like he said. I was negative as well.

I'd always had a condom policy, but this vacation was about being reckless, letting go, even adding some danger to my life, whatever it took to quiet the voices in my head. It was about escaping and not feeling the last three months. I was throwing caution completely out the window for the next three weeks and I didn't care that I might regret that decision later.

"I'm negative, too, Daddy. I want to feel you come inside of me."

"That's my good boy. Daddy is going to come in your sweet, tight ass and then watch as it drips out of you," he said as he started to pull the plug out of me.

I whined at the loss of the plug, but I knew it would soon be replaced by something so much better. I heard him open the lube and slick up before I felt his tip against my already stretched hole. The plug wasn't as thick as he was, but I didn't care. I didn't want him to stretch me any further. I wanted to feel the sting of him entering my hole. Of his dick stretching me out further. I couldn't stop moaning as his tip breached my hole and pushed inside of me. He felt so good. He was huge and this was exactly what I needed.

"So fucking big. Don't stop. I love the feel of the burn at first, Daddy." I groaned, hissing at the pain even as I pushed my hips back to get him to go even deeper inside of me.

He growled as he slammed his hips forward, pushing himself inside my ass all the way down to the base. I let out a small scream as the pain and pleasure mixed within my body. This man knew exactly what I needed and he wasn't afraid to give it to me.

And I loved it.

He was the perfect Daddy. He didn't give me any time to adjust before he pulled all the way back out to his tip, and then slammed right back inside of me, hitting my sweet spot dead on and making me scream out once again.

"Oh, Daddy, yes. Fuck me harder," I whimpered as he snapped his hips and drilled into me.

This man certainly didn't need to be told twice. He put his hands on my hips, his grip bruising, and started to pound into my hole like his life depended on it. I had no idea how long he was going to be able to last at this brutal pace, but I was hoping the fact that he already came once meant that he would be able to go long enough for me to come.

With each thrust, he hit my prostate and I saw stars. I couldn't stop moaning and whimpering at each thrust, each solid pass over my sweet spot. I was so hard I felt like I was going to explode soon.

"Oh yes, Daddy, don't stop. You're gonna make me come soon," I breathed out, panting deeply.

Daddy snaked his hand around my hip, wrapping his fist around my hard dick with a firm grip and it made me whimper at the sensation of his rough touch over my velvet skin.

"You're so hard, do you want Daddy to make you come?" he asked as he slowed his thrusts down to barely even moving.

"Yes please, Daddy, I need to come. Please make me come, Daddy. I'll do whatever you want," I easily begged. I knew that was what he wanted and I was all too happy to give it to him.

"Come for me. I want to feel your ass tighten around my cock," he ordered, as he started to jerk me off, pulling roughly at my cock yet still keeping his thrusts deep and slow.

He shifted his hips once more and I moaned at the contact of his dick hitting my sweet spot once again. It didn't take long before I let out a long, deep groan and came long and hard into his hand.

I heard Daddy moan as the walls of my ass tightened around him. I knew I was tight as I clamped down around his hardness. He had to stop moving so he wouldn't come yet. I was thankful for that, though, because I wanted to feel him inside of me longer.

When I stopped pulsing, he threaded

his free hand into my hair, fisting a chunk of it. He then pulled me up and back so I was on my knees with my back against his chest. He kept a tight grip on my hair and tilted my head back.

"Whatever I want, my sweet boy?" he asked, his voice a husky growl in my ear, sending shivers snaking down my spine.

"Yes, Daddy, anything."

Daddy held his cum covered hand up to me as he spoke. "Good boys always clean up their messes. Lick it clean."

"Yes, Daddy," I moaned, licking my lips. I took his hand in mine and brought it to my mouth. I started to lick up my own cum. I loved the taste of cum, even my own. I truly was a cock slut, but I was proud of it. At least in the bedroom.

"How does it taste, my boy?"

"Good, Daddy. I love the taste of cum,"

I whispered, pressing my ass back against his still hard dick, hoping he would take the hint that I was more than ready for more.

"Such a naughty, dirty slut you are. Daddy loves it," he said before he sucked hard on my neck, causing an appreciative moan to slip from my lips.

I loved being given hickies. I always felt like I was being marked and I loved that feeling. I loved feeling like I belonged to someone, that I had someone who wanted me enough to mark me as his.

Once Daddy's hand was clean, he pushed me back down onto the bed. He removed his hand from my hair and placed it on the back of my neck. Holding me down, he let go of all control and started to pound deep into my ass.

We were both a moaning mess and my

legs were trembling from the overwhelming pleasure my body was experiencing. Neither of us ever wanted this to end, that much was clear, but I could feel him getting closer, getting harder, swelling once more.

After a few more rapid thrusts, Daddy snapped his hips forward until he was balls deep inside of my ass and was coming with a loud groan. The second I felt his hot cum scorching the inside of my walls, I was whimpering and withering underneath him. I had never felt someone coming inside of me before and I instantly felt like I was being marked. That as long as his cum was inside of me, I belonged to him. That feeling alone had washed away the past three months. It removed that empty hole that I'd had inside of me. I knew it wouldn't last, but for right now, I felt complete bliss.

We were both breathing heavily and I already knew I could easily become addicted to him. I was hoping he was a local and we would be able to meet up again before I had to go back to New York. I needed this to be more than just a one-off.

I felt Daddy pulling out and I was disappointed that he wanted to watch the come drip out of me. I wanted to keep it there a bit longer. To my surprise, though, I felt the plug being pushed back inside of me as he spoke.

"I like the idea of you walking around with my cum inside of you."

"Me too, Daddy." I instantly said, and it was the complete truth. I didn't want the feeling of belonging to him to disappear just yet. I wanted to embrace it just a bit longer. I *needed* to.

He removed his hand from the back of my neck and I felt him climbing off of the bed. I knew we were finished for the night, but I was really hoping we could meet up again. I was hoping he would want that, too.

"You a local?" he asked.

"No, just visiting for three weeks, Daddy," I said as I moved and started to get dressed.

"Care to meet up again, my sweet boy?" He pulled his jeans up over his thick hips and buttoned them closed as he gazed at me, a cat that ate the cream look on his face.

"Definitely," I easily agreed, flashing him a smile.

He pulled out his phone and handed it to me as he spoke. "Give Daddy your number."

"Yes, Daddy."

I took the offered phone and typed in my number before I handed it back to him. I'd let him decide on what he was going to put the number under.

Once he had my number saved, he tucked the phone away into his pocket as he spoke in that husky voice of his. I couldn't help but wonder if maybe he smoked for it to get that way.

"When Daddy texts you, you will answer and you will meet me when I tell you. Do I make myself clear?"

"Yes, Daddy. I'll be a good boy," I promised. For now, at least. I was extremely interested in seeing what a punishment by this man would feel like.

"You better or Daddy will punish you. You go straight back to your hotel room.

COOPER

You won't let anyone touch you while you are in town. You belong to me until you go back home. Do I make myself clear?" he ordered and damn, didn't that almost have me fully hard again.

"Yes, Daddy. I only belong to you."

He didn't say anything else. He simply turned and strolled out the door.

I let out a shaky breath as I tried to get my emotions back under control. That man had a way of making me feel pleasure on a whole new level. He knew exactly what I needed and he gave me more than what I could ever have hoped for. I had no idea who he was or when he would text me, but I was hoping I would be seeing him again tomorrow. I only had three weeks down here and I wanted to spend every chance I could with that man.

EVIE RILEY

Watch for Noah at your favorite online
retailer!

OTHER BOOKS BY EVIE

Federal Protection Agency
Mason
Rafe
Ryzen
Cooper
Noah
Damien
Sebastian
Gabe
Logan

Ruthless Empire
Courting Danger
Chasing Danger
Kissing Danger

Smokejumpers
Hawke
Cyrus
Jase
Gage
Jackson
Xavier

EVIE RILEY

Jasper Springs
Cade
Dawson
Drew
Grayson
Riley
Mitch

From The Edge
Shattered
Runaway
Jaded
Rescue
Hidden
Tormented

Gray Vale Pack
His Fated Mate
His Wounded Warrior
His Healing Heart

ABOUT THE AUTHOR

Evie Riley is a prolific, neurodivergent author known for her captivating MM romance novels. She has gained a significant following and topped the LGBT+ action and adventure bestseller charts with her series.

Evie's writing style often explores dark and gritty themes where her men must overcome difficult obstacles in their search for love, but she has also ventured into sweeter small-town romances, incorporating tropes like enemies-to-lovers, friends-to-lovers, age-gap, and forced proximity. She is known for crafting engaging romantic suspense novels and has a knack for creating interconnected series worlds that keep readers invested.

EVIE RILEY

Interestingly, Ms. Riley has hinted at exploring new genres, such as Alien Omegaverse Romance, in the future.

Outside of writing, she enjoys spending time at the beach and has a quirky personality, described by her partner as ranging from cute to deadly, depending on her blood-chocolate levels.

Evie spends her nights writing bad boys in love, and her days wrangling the sweet boys she loves.